***"I know how to defend myself, Detective O'Brien,"*** he informed her tersely.

"Good, then this shouldn't be a difficult assignment for me."

Blake tried again. "My father was a marine."

Greer forced a smile to her lips. "So you said."

"The point of my reference is that he insisted on teaching me self-defense," he told her.

"Well, unless he also taught you how to catch bullets with your bare hands, I'm afraid you still need me."

"This whole situation is ridiculous," he ground out.

She sighed. "Judge, I've been assigned to you, so you might as well make the best of it." She added pointedly, "I promise to be as unobtrusive as possible. You'll hardly notice I'm there."

There was silence for a moment. Greer slanted a look in Kincannon's direction and instantly became aware of his eyes moving over her slowly, as if to take the measure of every inch of her.

"Oh," the judge r
doubt that...."

Dear Reader,

Welcome back to the *Cavanaugh Justice* series. This time around, we have Greer O'Brien's story. Greer and her two brothers are the illegitimate offspring of the late Mike Cavanaugh, Andrew and Brian's malcontented brother. Like her brothers, Greer thought that her father was a fallen hero, not a man who refused to live up to his responsibilities. Her mother's deathbed confession has actually hit her hard. It makes her resolve never to lose her heart to a male of the species, because men disappoint the women who love them.

But this is before she is given an assignment she would rather pass on: being the bodyguard for Judge Blake Kincannon, whose life is threatened by an escaped drug dealer. She and Blake have a history. Despite this, the two become aware of the strong attraction humming between them, an attraction neither one can continue to deny.

I hope you like this latest installment in the Cavanaugh saga and as always, I thank you for reading my book. From the bottom of my heart, I wish you someone to love who loves you back.

*Marie Ferrarella*

# MARIE FERRARELLA

## *Cavanaugh Judgment*

ROMANTIC
*SUSPENSE*

**SILHOUETTE BOOKS**

ISBN-13: 978-0-373-27682-0

CAVANAUGH JUDGMENT

Copyright © 2010 by Marie Rydzynski-Ferrarella

**Printed in U.S.A.**

## MARIE FERRARELLA

This *USA TODAY* bestselling and RITA® Award-winning author has written almost two hundred novels for Silhouette Books, some under the name Marie Nicole. Her romances are beloved by fans worldwide. Visit her Web site at www.marieferrarella.com.

To
Lily Sterkel.
Welcome to the world,
little one.

# Chapter 1

Eddie Munro was the kind of man who reminded narcotics detective Greer O'Brien of the Aurora police department why she'd joined the force in the first place. To put low-life scum like him away.

The least acrimonious way to describe Munro was to say that he was a career criminal with a rap sheet that was longer than he was tall and, at five feet eleven inches, that was saying a great deal. There apparently was no hint of remorse in the man's heart, no well-buried twinge of guilt associated with any of the victims who he had harmed during his ambitious climb up the drug-dealing ladder. He was, and always had been, the most important person in his universe.

Greer could tell that simply by looking into the drug dealer's eyes. They were flat, cold and calculating, and could have just as easily belonged to a reptile as to a flesh and blood human being. She saw it now, in the courtroom, and she'd seen it then, when the sting she'd been part of had gone down, successfully snaring Munro in its net. They were dead eyes, silently telling her that this arrest was merely a temporary aberration, an obstacle to be surmounted.

He looked, she thought, as if he had some secret guarantee that he would be out again soon, pushing his people to hook naïve, thoughtless teenagers in search of diversion on drugs, eventually turning large numbers of them into wraithlike creatures willing to sell what was left of their souls for the next fix.

Greer could see that same look in Munro's eyes now, as she looked at him across the marginally populated courtroom. He was sitting at the defense table, dressed in a suit his attorney was hoping would transform him from a minor kingpin in the organization into a respectable-looking member of society.

But nothing could transform his eyes. They were looking at her and there was murderous contempt in the brown orbs.

Contempt and more than a small amount of anger that he was being inconvenienced this way.

It made Greer long—just for the tiniest of seconds—for the days of vigilante justice that had thrived in the Wild West before law and order had prevailed. Because vigilante justice would have disposed of worthless creeps like Munro without so much as a fleeting second thought.

There were no second chances with vigilante justice.

But even as she thought it, Greer knew in her heart that if such a thing as vigilante justice was alive and well, she would have been part of the first line of defense against it. It was inherently in her blood to uphold the law.

But that didn't mean she didn't find this whole tedious "due process" of crossing *t*'s and dotting *i*'s trying, she thought irritably.

Because it wasn't enough to catch vermin like Eddie Munro in the act and arrest him. He had to be convicted, as well—and that was always tricky. Despite the fact that the man was as guilty as sin, conviction was never a foregone conclusion, because there were lawyers involved. Lawyers who earned their fees—and possibly a rush, as well—by digging through technicalities, searching for that one little "something" that had been overlooked, some obscure loophole that would somehow serve to set the Eddie Munros of the world back on the street to prey on the defenseless.

The need to present the case against him and prosecute Munro to the full measure of the law was why she was here, sitting in a place she avoided like the plague whenever possible. More than half an hour ago she had solemnly sworn to "tell the truth, the whole truth and nothing but the truth so help me, God." She would have willingly sworn to almost anything if it meant locking away one more evil vulture for as long as legally possible.

It wasn't that courtrooms—or testifying—made her nervous. What they did was make her angry. Angry because, like it or not, all the hard work that she and the men and women she worked with in the narcotics division could be thrown out on one of those aforementioned technicalities. One overzealous movement by a wet-behind-the-ears rookie cop could jeopardize months of hard work.

But she knew that this was part of the game, part of the system, and she was determined to do everything she could to put that soulless pseudo Drug Czar of Magnolia Avenue, as Munro liked to refer to himself, away. She would have preferred putting him away for good, but ultimately, she would take what she could get. Every day Munro wasn't on the street was another day someone else potentially avoided becoming addicted.

Greer was well aware that every victory counted, no matter how small.

The sound of a door sighing closed registered and she glanced toward the back of the courtroom, just in time to see the chief of detectives, Brian Cavanaugh, make his way down the far aisle and slip into one of the near-empty middle rows.

*What was up?*

Greer couldn't help wondering if the well-respected chief was here because of the case in general, or because his daughter, Janelle Cavanaugh-Boone, was the assistant district attorney prosecuting this case.

Or if, by some remote chance, he was here to lend her his support. Brian Cavanaugh was, after all, her newfound uncle.

The thought would have coaxed an ironic smile to her lips if the overall situation hadn't been so grave. And if she wasn't currently on the stand, testifying and being relentlessly grilled by Munro's defense attorney, Hayden Wells, an oily little man who, despite his posturing, was not all that good at his job.

The latter discovery—that Brian Cavanaugh was her uncle, that she, Kyle and Ethan were actually related to the numerous Cavanaughs who populated the police force—still boggled her mind a bit, as she was fairly certain it did her brothers. Triplets, they tended to feel more or less the same about the bigger issues that affected their lives and learning that they had been lied to by their mother all their lives was about as big an issue as there was.

It was only on their mother's deathbed that the twenty-six-year-old triplets learned that the man they had believed was their late father, a war hero killed on foreign shores nobly defending freedom, never even existed. He had been created by Jane O'Brien in order to make her children feel wanted and normal. In truth, they were conceived during a brief liaison between Mike Cavanaugh, the sullen black sheep of an otherwise highly respected family, and their mother, a woman who had fallen hopelessly in love with the brooding policeman.

Angry, hurt, bewildered, the day after the funeral Kyle had marched up to Andrew Cavanaugh, the former chief of police and family patriarch, and dropped the bombshell that there were three more Cavanaughs than initially accounted for on the man's doorstep.

Rather than rejection and scorn, which was what she knew Kyle was expecting, she and her brothers had found acceptance. Not wholesale, at least, not at first, but rather swiftly down the line, all things considered.

Taken in by the family, that left Greer and her brothers to work out their own feelings regarding the tsunamic shift that their lives had suddenly experienced. To some extent, they were still wrestling. But at least the angst was gone.

Pacing before the witness stand as he addressed her, Munro's defense attorney paused. The slight involuntary twitch of his lips indicated that he wasn't satisfied with the way his round of questioning was going. At the outset, it seemed as if he was winning, but now that conclusion was no longer cast in stone. The balding attorney's voice rose as his confidence decreased.

The momentary lull allowed Greer to shift her eyes to the side row again. She was surprised to make eye contact with the chief of detectives. And even more surprised to see the smile of approval that rose to his lips.

He mouthed, "Good job," and at first, she assumed that Brian had intended the commendation for his daughter's efforts. But Janelle had her back to the rear of the courtroom—and her father.

The approval was intended for her.

Greer realized that a smile was slowly spreading across her own lips. She'd always told herself that, like her brothers, she was her own person and that approval didn't matter.

But it did.

She could feel the warmth that approval created spreading through her, taking hold. Ever so slightly, she nodded her head in acknowledgment of her superior. Of her uncle.

The next moment, she heard the judge's gavel come down on her right. Her attention returned to the immediate proceedings.

Alert, Greer waited to hear what the judge had to say, trying not to dwell on the fact that she was sitting far closer than was comfortable to Judge Blake Kincannon.

It wasn't that she had anything against Kincannon— she didn't. In her opinion, Aurora's youngest judge on the bench was everything that a model judge was supposed to be. Fair, impartial, compassionate—but not a bleeding heart—he was the kind of judge who actually made her believe that maybe, just maybe, the system could actually work. At least some of the time.

Added to that, Blake Kincannon even *looked* like the picture of a model judge. Tall, imposing, with chiseled features, piercing blue eyes and hair blacker than the inside of a harden criminal's heart, Kincannon was considered to be outstandingly handsome and quite a catch for those who were in the "catching" business.

No, Greer's discomfort arose for an entirely different reason.

She was certain that whenever Judge Blake Kincannon looked at her, he remembered. Remembered that she was the patrol officer who had been first on the scene of the car accident two years ago. Remembered that she was the one who had tried, unsuccessfully, to administer CPR to his wife as she lay dying. And remembered that she was the one who, when he regained consciousness at the hospital after the doctors had stabilized him, broke the news to him that his wife was dead.

Not exactly something a man readily put out of his mind, she'd thought when Detective Jeff Carson, her partner for the past year, had told her who the presiding judge on the case was going to be.

She'd been dreading walking into the courtroom for months. And now, hopefully, it was almost over.

The sound of the gavel focused attention on the judge. All eyes were on him. Kincannon waited until the courtroom was quiet again.

"I think that this might be a good place to call a recess for lunch." The judge's deep voice rumbled like thunder over the parched plains of late summer. And then he glanced in her direction, his eyes only fleetingly touching hers. "You are dismissed, Detective. The court thanks you for your testimony."

*But I'm sure you would rather it had come from someone else,* Greer couldn't help thinking even as she inclined her head in acknowledgment.

She rose to her feet at the same time that Kincannon did.

And then the commotion erupted so quickly, it took Greer a while to piece it all together later that day.

One moment, the courtroom was buzzing with the semi-subdued rustle of spectators gathering themselves and their things together in order to leave the premises, the next, terrified screams and cries pierced the air.

And then there was the sound of a gun being discharged.

But the tiny half heartbeat in between the two occurrences was what actually counted.

Greer had immediately glanced away from Kincannon the moment their eyes made contact when the judge dismissed her. Which as it turned out, she later reflected, was exceedingly fortunate for the judge. Because if she hadn't looked away, she wouldn't have seen Munro leap up to his feet and simultaneously push the defense table over, sending the table and everything on it crashing to the floor. That created a diversion just long enough for Munro, in his respectable suit, to lunge at the approaching bailiff, drive a fist to the man's gut and grab the doubled-over bailiff's weapon.

"Gun!" Greer yelled and, in what felt like one swift, unending motion, she leaped up onto the witness stand chair where she had just been sitting a second ago, propelled herself onto the judge's desk and hurled herself into the judge, sending the surprised Kincannon crashing down to the floor behind his desk.

Scrambling, she was quick to cover his body with her own.

The desk obstructing her view, Greer heard rather than saw what was going on next. There was the sound of terror, of people yelling and running and ducking for cover. And then there was the sound of a gun being discharged again—one round. Whether the gun belonged to the other bailiff or was the one that Munro had seized from the first bailiff she had no idea.

At this point, everything was registering somewhere on the outer perimeter of her consciousness.

What she was *acutely* aware of was that she was lying

spread-eagle over the judge, that he was on his back and she was on his front. And that all the parts that counted were up close and personal.

The infusion of adrenaline sailing in triple time through her body had her heart racing so hard she was certain that some kind of a record was being set. Greer felt hot and cold and light-headed all at the same time, a reaction definitely *not* typical of her. She struggled to regain control over herself and her surroundings.

Her eyes met Kincannon's. As if suddenly pulled into the belly of an industrial vacuum cleaner, all the noise and chaos surrounding them seemed to have faded into oblivion for just the slightest increment of a second.

And then she blinked.

"How long have you been under the illusion that you're bulletproof, Detective O'Brien?" Kincannon asked her gruffly.

The question instantly pulled her back into the eye of the courtroom hurricane. "I'm not," she heard herself answering.

"Then what are you doing on top of me?"

"Saving your life, Your Honor," she snapped.

Her heart slowed down to a mere double time. There was a criminal to subdue. The thought telegraphed itself through her brain. Greer scrambled up to her feet. As did the judge.

"Stay down!" she ordered sharply, circumventing his desk.

Kincannon clearly had no intention of being ordered around or of staying down, cowering behind his desk. His court had just been disrespected. The judge stood directly behind her, his robe billowing out on the sides like some fantasy superhero's cape.

"My courtroom," Kincannon informed her, raising his voice above the din, "my rules."

His courtroom, Greer noted as she swiftly scanned the area, taking everything in, was in utter chaos. It was also apparently missing one felon. The second gunshot that had rung out *had* come from the purloined weapon, and the bullet—whether intentionally or not—had hit the bailiff whose weapon had been stolen by Munro. The latter, on the job all of six months, was on the floor, clutching his shoulder. Blood was seeping out between his fingers.

Munro was nowhere to be seen.

Inside a secured courtroom with law enforcement officers throughout the building, Munro had done the impossible. The drug dealer had escaped.

A glance to the left told her the chief of detectives was missing, as well.

For one terrifying moment, an utterly unacceptable scenario suggested itself to her, but she dismissed it. Brian Cavanaugh was too much of a policeman to have ever allowed himself to be taken hostage. If Munro had even attempted it, she was certain the dealer would have been lying on the floor in several disjointed pieces.

The man would have instinctively known that avoiding the chief at all costs was the only way he was going to make it out of the courthouse alive.

Greer refused to believe that Munro had already gotten out of the building. Not enough time had gone by.

She ran through the double doors that led out of the

courtroom into the hallway. She didn't have to look over her shoulder to know Kincannon was right behind her. Did the man have a death wish? she wondered, annoyed.

There was more chaos beyond the leather padded doors. People, fleeing for their lives, were hiding in alcoves, pressed as far against the beige walls as humanly possible in an attempt to avoid the escaping criminal's attention.

*Damn it, things like this just don't happen,* Greer thought angrily.

Except that it just had.

She scanned the hallway again, hoping that she'd missed something. Hoping that Munro was trying to hide in plain sight. But he wasn't.

At first glance, it appeared that Eddie Munro had turned out to be far cleverer than she'd initially thought. The drug dealer had managed to disappear.

She saw the chief. He was standing a few feet away and had taken charge of the bailiffs who had come running in response to the gunshot. On the phone, he'd already put in a call for reinforcements.

"I want everything shut down," he ordered the uniformed men and women gathered around him. "Except for my people, nobody leaves, nobody comes in. Understand?"

Acquiescing murmurs responded to his words.

He looked at the bailiffs. "I want every courtroom, every office, every closet on every floor gone through." His penetrating look swept over the collective. "Do it in teams. I don't want anyone caught off guard. One damn surprise is enough for the day. You—" he singled out the closest bailiff "—call for an ambulance. I want that bailiff who got shot attended to."

The man rushed off to place the call. As the other men and women he'd just addressed scattered, Brian turned his attention to Greer. His eyes swept over her, taking full measure. Looking for a wound. Finding none, he still asked, "Are you all right, Greer?"

Self-conscious at being singled out this way—did he think she couldn't take care of herself?—Greer dismissed the concern she heard in her superior's voice. "I'm fine, Chief." And then she couldn't help herself. She had to know. "Why are you asking?"

He laughed shortly, shaking his head. "Well, for one thing," he began wryly, "I saw you take that half-gainer over the judge's desk—"

"She had a soft landing," Kincannon told him as he came up to the chief.

Greer shifted slightly. "Not so soft," she muttered under her breath. She'd been acutely aware of every single contour she'd come in contact with and *soft* was not the word that readily came to mind.

Calling out to Janelle, who he saw hurrying out of the courtroom and looking around, Brian didn't appear to have heard Greer's comment.

But the judge did.

# Chapter 2

Greer turned around. The moment she did, her eyes met Kincannon's.

He'd heard her. She was certain of it.

What she didn't know was how he'd received the offhand comment that had just slipped out. Was that a hint of amusement she saw on his face, or was it something else? She'd never been around the man in one of his lighter moments—didn't even know if he *had* lighter moments—so she couldn't gauge what was going on in his head right now.

Talk about awkward, she thought. And it was of her own making. Someday, she was going to learn to think before she spoke, or at least that was what her brothers were always saying to her.

"Someday, that mouth of yours is going to get you

in a whole lot of trouble," Ethan had warned her more than once.

She could take that kind of a comment from Ethan far more easily than she could from Kyle. From Kyle, it sounded more like criticism. Besides, she was closer to Ethan than to Kyle, which was odd, given that the three of them had drawn their first breaths less than seven minutes apart. According to birth order, Kyle was technically the "oldest," then her, then Ethan. "The baby," their mother used to fondly call him.

Kyle had called him that, as well, until Ethan had given Kyle his first black eye. The word *baby* hadn't come up again in approximately sixteen years.

None of that changed the fact that her brothers were both right. She had a tendency to let her thoughts reach her lips, completely bypassing her brain. Most of the time, it didn't matter. But most of the time she didn't find herself on top of a judge who had a rock-solid body hidden beneath his imposing black robes.

Raising her chin, Greer stoically waited to be upbraided for her comment regarding the judge's body. Instead, without so much as uttering a word, Kincannon turned on his heel and made his way back into the courtroom.

Was she off the hook?

Or was he planning on denouncing her formally later on? Her experience with judges, as with lawyers, had not yielded a great deal of positive reinforcement.

"Greer." The chief's voice cut through the din in the hall. She turned around to face him, waiting to be dispatched where she could do the most good. Brian motioned toward the courtroom. "Stay with him," he instructed.

Greer opened her mouth to protest that she would be more useful looking for the prisoner, but then she shut it again, for once keeping her words to herself. She knew better than to argue with authority, even with someone as genial and affable as the chief. She wasn't about to abuse the fact that he was her uncle. Years ago in the school yard, she'd learned the wisdom of picking her battles judiciously.

"Yes, Chief." The sound of numerous feet running toward them told her that the officers Brian had sent for had arrived. She'd already turned away and was hurrying back into the courtroom. Behind her, she heard Brian continue to organize the search for Munro.

Greer wouldn't have wanted to be in the drug dealer's shoes when Brian found him for any amount of money in the world.

Entering the courtroom, she noted that it was mostly empty. She glanced toward Kincannon's desk.

He wasn't there.

Before her adrenaline had the opportunity to ramp up, she spotted the judge on the floor. He was kneeling beside the wounded bailiff.

Coming closer, Greer saw that the bottom of the judge's robe was torn and ragged. Though she hadn't thought it was possible, Kincannon had somehow managed to tear a long strip off his robe and was now using it to form a tourniquet for the wounded bailiff. Moreover, he was doing it himself rather than instructing the other bailiff to do it.

Admiration stirred within her. Too often judges thought themselves above the people they interacted with. Nice to know that wasn't a hard and fast rule.

"Lie flat, Tim," Kincannon told the bailiff when the injured man tried to sit up.

So he knew him, she thought. From the job or from somewhere else?

To underscore his words, the judge put the flat of his hand against the young bailiff's blood-soaked shirt and exerted just enough pressure to make the man remain down. In his weakened state, Tim could offer no real resistance.

Joining them, Greer squatted down beside the judge as she looked at the bailiff. "Better do as he says if you ever want to work in his courtroom again," she advised with an encouraging smile.

Tim looked like a kid, she thought. She did her best to sound upbeat for the bailiff's sake. He looked scared and he'd lost a lot of blood. She was rather surprised that Tim was still conscious, much less making an attempt to sit up.

"Nice work," she said to Kincannon, nodding at the tourniquet he'd fashioned. She slanted a glance in his direction, forcing herself not to look away too quickly. "Let me guess, you earned a merit badge in first aid when you were a kid."

Blake secured the ends of the strip as best he could. *That should hold until the paramedics get here,* he thought.

Sitting back on his heels, he continued to maintain eye contact with the frightened bailiff. He couldn't remember ever being that young. It seemed to Blake that somehow, through a trick of fate, he'd been born old.

"Nothing wrong with being an Eagle Scout," he responded.

"Wow, an Eagle Scout." Somehow, she had envisioned Kincannon being more of a rebel. Not too much call for rebels in the Boy Scouts. When he looked at her quizzically, she explained, "My brother Kyle only lasted a month in the Cub Scouts."

Kincannon continued looking at her. "Let me guess, he didn't think the rules applied to him."

Kyle *never* thought the rules applied to him. He made his own as he went along.

Of course, all that was going to change soon. Kyle had actually found his soul mate and was planning on getting married.

Who would have ever thought…?

Greer lifted a shoulder in a semi-shrug. "Something like that."

"Family trait?" Kincannon mused.

Greer looked at him. To ask that, the judge would have had to be familiar with her family. Granted, she and her brothers were all detectives with the Aurora police department, but she was not so self-centered as to think that the world revolved around her family. Besides, she usually kept a low profile.

She wanted to know his reasoning. "Why would you say that?"

"I'm a fairly good judge of character, no pun intended." He gave his handiwork a once-over to make sure it was secure. Satisfied, he nodded to himself. But rather than standing up, Kincannon looked at the woman beside him for a long moment. "Rather than duck out of range, the way everyone else in the courtroom did, you jumped on my desk, making yourself the most visible target in the room."

Her eyes narrowed just a little, even as she told herself not to take offense. She hadn't expected him to thank her profusely, but neither had she expected him to take her to task for it, either.

"With all due respect, Your Honor, I didn't exactly break into a tap dance, searching for my fifteen seconds of fame. I jumped on the desk because it was the fastest way to get you out of harm's way."

"It's fifteen minutes, not seconds," he corrected mildly, "and at thirty-four, I'm perfectly capable of getting out of harm's way on my own."

Greer squared her shoulders. *Infected with a little hubris, are we?* It looked as if she might just have to revise her opinion of Kincannon. Again.

"I'm assuming, Your Honor, that at thirty-four, your eyesight is still twenty-twenty."

Rather than answer in the affirmative, Kincannon's eyes held hers as he rose to his feet. "What are you getting at?"

She was in no hurry to blurt out her answer. "That Munro discharged the weapon twice. The second bullet went into the bailiff you just bandaged."

His eyes never left hers. Even so, there wasn't even the slightest hint as to what was going on in his head.

Was he taking offense, highly amused or just giving her enough rope in hopes that she'd hang herself?

*Not today, Judge.*

"You're going to tell me about the first bullet, aren't you?" he asked, his tone mild.

"Absolutely," she said cheerfully. Greer marched over to Kincannon's desk and rounded it, going directly to the wall behind it. He followed. She pointed to an area that was the exact same height as his throat was from the floor. Her meaning was clear. Had he been standing where he'd been a moment longer, he wouldn't have been with them now. "You were his first target."

Blake dismissed her conclusion with an indifferent shrug. "Coincidence."

Greer suppressed an annoyed sigh. So he was thick-headed. Maybe the bullet wouldn't have penetrated after all.

This wasn't the time to get into an argument, she told herself silently. There was nothing to be gained by butting heads with this man. Her energy could be better spent otherwise.

But that still didn't keep her from looking as if she was merely humoring him. She inclined her head like an acquiescing servant. "Have it your way."

Rather than taking her tone as confrontational, he murmured, "I usually do."

*I just bet you do.*

Greer pressed her lips together in a physical effort to keep a retort from making it out into the open. It wasn't easy.

But before she could give in to the urge to break

her silence, the doors to the courtroom were thrown open and two uniformed paramedics, pushing a gurney between them, hurried into the room.

"He's over here," Kincannon called out to the duo, beckoning the men over as he made his way over to the bailiff. They reached Tim at the same time. The wounded bailiff was no longer bleeding, thanks to the tourniquet, but he was exceedingly pale. "One shot to the chest," Blake told them. "The bullet's still inside. I just applied the tourniquet a couple of minutes ago."

The paramedic closest to him nodded at the information as he appeared to make a quick assessment of the makeshift bandage.

"Nice job, Judge," the man commented approvingly. His partner released the brakes that were holding the gurney upright. The mobile stretcher instantly collapsed like a fainting patient. "We're going to shift you onto the gurney, sir," the first paramedic told Tim. "It's going to hurt a bit," he warned.

Tim looked as if he was struggling to remain conscious. He moaned. His expression indicated that he had no idea where the sound was coming from.

"On three," the first paramedic instructed. The other paramedic fumbled slightly, bumping Tim's shoulders against the corner of the gurney. It earned him a black look from his partner. "Good help's hard to find these days," he commented, addressing his words to the judge.

Once Tim was on the gurney and strapped in, the two paramedics snapped the stretcher into its upright position again. "Let's get that wound looked at," the first paramedic said to Tim. With his partner, they began to maneuver the gurney back to the double doors.

"Judge," Tim suddenly called out, his voice weak and cracking.

Three quick strides had Kincannon catching up to the gurney. He trotted to keep up alongside Tim. The paramedics never stopped, never even slowed down.

The wound was undoubtedly more serious than first anticipated, Blake thought. Looking down at the bailiff's face, he asked, "What is it, Tim?"

Tim pressed his lips together. Were they trembling? Greer wondered as she followed beside Kincannon. And why was the bailiff looking at the paramedics as if he was terrified? Her next thought was that the young man was probably afraid. No one applied for the job thinking they'd get shot.

"I'm sorry," Tim was saying, then repeated, "I'm sorry."

Blake put his own interpretation to the apology. Tim was sorry that he hadn't been able to stop the prisoner from escaping. Blake squeezed the wounded bailiff's good hand reassuringly. "Don't worry, Tim, we'll get him. I promise."

There wasn't so much as a shred of doubt in the man's voice, Greer thought. Either Kincannon had a hell of a lot more confidence in the system and in the department's ability to track Munro down for a second time than she did, or he was just naïve.

Kincannon didn't look like a naïve man.

But then, she thought, smart people were fooled all the time. Look at her and her brothers. They'd been unwittingly duped for twenty-six years by the one person they had all loved unconditionally. That kind of thing shook up your faith in the world and made you reassess all your existing values and views.

Offering the wounded man an encouraging smile, Kincannon slipped his hand out of Tim's fingers. The judge dropped back as the two paramedics swiftly whisked the wounded bailiff through the double doors and out into the hall.

He walked like a man who owned his destiny and his surroundings, Greer thought, watching him cross back to her. Maybe he'd gotten over his wife's death and moved on. For his sake, she certainly hoped so. The man she remembered encountering in the hospital had been all but broken.

"You probably saved his life," Greer said as Kincannon came closer to her.

"You save some, you lose some." The remark appeared to be directed more to himself than to her.

Okay, maybe he *wasn't* over his wife. What else could his response mean? Did the judge blame her for not being able to save the woman? God knew she'd tried, doing compressions and breathing into the woman's mouth until she thought she'd pass out herself.

Greer could feel words of protest rising to her lips. Again she pressed them together. This definitely wasn't the time to get into that. Besides, the judge hadn't actually come out and *said* anything to accuse her. Maybe she was just being paranoid.

As she was trying to decide whether or not she was overreacting, she saw Kincannon make his way over to

Munro's attorney. The small, slight man looked very shaken. His hands trembled as he attempted to pack up his briefcase. Twice papers slipped out of his hands, falling to the table and onto the floor like giant, dirty snowflakes.

"Until I'm persuaded otherwise, I'm holding you responsible for Munro's escape, Mr. Wells," Kincannon said to the man.

In response, Hayden Wells abandoned his briefcase and began stuttering, unraveling right in front of them.

"I didn't— I wouldn't—" All but hyperventilating, Wells cleared his throat and tried again. "Your Honor, you can't be serious."

Greer saw the steely look that came into the judge's eyes. She certainly wouldn't have wanted to be on the receiving end of that, she thought.

"I can," Kincannon informed him, "and I am."

"But, Judge," Wells squeaked, his voice cracking out of sheer fear, "I had no way of knowing that this was going to happen. No way," he insisted. "I'm just as surprised as you are."

"I sincerely doubt that," Blake responded coldly.

Reining in his frustration, he set his jaw hard. This shouldn't have happened, he thought. There were supposed to be safeguards in place. Were all the security measures just a sham?

Taking a deep breath, ignoring the babbling lawyer, Blake slowly looked around the empty courtroom.

Frustration ate away at him. He sincerely regretted his own ruling which had specifically forbidden any videotaping of proceedings. At the time his thinking had been that he didn't want tapes to be leaked to the media, didn't want cases to be compromised because some reporter wanted to break a story.

But in this case, if there *had* been a video camera on, it would have caught the events preceding Munro's escape on tape and that would have been a godsend. Blake had a gut feeling that Munro hadn't acted alone. This wasn't a spur-of-the-moment thing. The man had to have had help. A *lot* of help. Blake was willing to bet a year's salary on it.

Wells was still sputtering that he was offended that someone of the judge's caliber would actually think that he would lower himself to aid a criminal.

"I could be disbarred!" he declared dramatically.

Greer had a feeling the man was just warming up. She was about to tell him to keep quiet when Kincannon beat her to it.

"Please spare me your self-righteous protests, Mr. Wells. I am well aware of your record. No one enters my courtroom without my knowing his background," he told the man. "Someone who loses as often as you do can't possibly support himself in this line of work without having something else going on on the side."

Wells's dark eyebrows rose all the way up his very large forehead, all but meeting the semicircle of fringe that surrounded the back of his head. "Your Honor, I give you my word—"

Greer didn't know how much more they could take. "That and two dollars will get you a ride on the bus," she observed.

Damn, she'd done it again, Greer thought. That wasn't supposed to have come out. Not because she didn't mean it, but because she had no idea how Kincannon would react to her flippant attitude.

But when her eyes met his, if anything, Kincannon appeared to be somewhat amused. Or, at the very least, in agreement.

"My sentiments exactly," he told her.

The din just beyond the double doors in the hallway suddenly increased, swelling to three times its original decibel level.

Hopefully, there was only one reason for that. "Maybe they found him," Greer guessed, looking at Kincannon. With that, she decided to see for herself. Moving quickly, Greer hurried out the double doors to find out. She'd intended to report back.

She should have known better. Apparently Kincannon didn't like to remain stationary.

"Maybe," she heard him agree, then add, "You stay here." Since she was all but out the door, he had to be addressing the order to Wells. "I want to have a few more words with you when I get back."

Greer stopped dead the second she was out the doors.

There were two paramedics in the hallway. Two paramedics pushing a gurney.

A feeling of déjà vu slid over her. That and a great deal of uneasy confusion.

She wasn't the only one experiencing it.

Even before Greer reached the paramedics, she had

a sinking feeling in the pit of her stomach. Something was terribly off.

The lead paramedic looked only slightly friendlier than a rattlesnake.

"Look, we got the call and got here as fast as we could. MacArthur Boulevard's a parking lot," he bit off, his words directed at the chief. "Now, is there a patient or isn't there? We're short-handed and we don't have any time for some damn game."

Instead of answering the man, Brian put in a call to dispatch.

"Yeah, Hallie, it's Chief Cavanaugh. How many ambulances did you send out?" He listened to the answer. "Okay, describe the paramedics." He frowned. "What do you mean you can't keep track?"

"Chief," Greer interrupted, pushing her way through the crowd. "Let me send her a picture so she can identify them," she suggested.

Brian paused. He looked at his cell phone uncertainly, then lifted his eyes to Greer's. "Does this—?"

She nodded, knowing what he was going to ask, sparing him the embarrassment of having to put it into words. "Yes, it does," she assured him. Taking his phone, she snapped a shot of the two disgruntled-looking paramedics. Done, she quickly forwarded it to the woman on the other end of the line, then handed the cell phone back to the chief.

Confirmation was almost immediate.

"You didn't send another team?" Brian knew the answer before he even asked the question. His mouth was grim as he muttered, "Thanks."

Flipping the phone closed, Brian regarded the officers gathered around him. The paramedics were all but forgotten. "Right under our noses," he declared, his voice low and steely.

He made Greer think of a volcano that was trying not to erupt.

# Chapter 3

Confused, Blake looked from the chief of detectives to the animated narcotics detective at his side. It was now a foregone conclusion that the first set of paramedics who'd whisked Timothy Kelly away had been bogus. However, the rest of it didn't make sense to him.

"But why would they kidnap the bailiff? If they were in on the escape, wouldn't they have found a way to make off with Munro?" he asked.

*Who said they didn't?* Greer thought as she shook her head. "They didn't kidnap the bailiff, the bailiff was part of it."

Blake refused to believe it. He could remember Tim's first day on the job. So obviously wet behind the ears, the young bailiff had been so eager to please, so eager to do a good job, it had almost been painful to watch. "But they almost killed him," he protested.

Brian was clearly struggling to keep his temper under control. "*Almost* being the operative word," the chief pointed out.

"No, you're wrong," Kincannon insisted. "I know the man. He's shown me photographs of his wife, of his baby daughter. A man like that doesn't suddenly get up one morning and decide to help a career felon escape out of a courtroom."

He was having trouble with this, Greer realized. Rather than instantly become indignant because he'd been duped, Kincannon was searching for some elusive reason that would explain what happened and absolve the bailiff of any wrongdoing beyond being in the wrong place at the wrong time. She had to grudgingly admit she found that admirable. At the very least, that made the judge more of a human being than most who sat on the bench.

Reviewing the situation, she realized that there was possibly a plausible explanation that could be acceptable to both sides. The more she thought about it, the more it seemed to fit. She sincerely doubted that Kincannon could be easily deceived.

"Maybe he didn't just wake up one morning and decide to help a hardened felon escape," she suggested, her conviction growing stronger with each word. "Maybe Tim Kelly had no choice."

Janelle had been quiet this entire time, remaining out of her father's way as he took charge of the situation. But now she seemed compelled to point out the obvious flaw in her new cousin's theory. "They weren't holding a gun to his head, Greer," she said, her tone of voice barely masking the frustration she clearly felt over the drug dealer's escape.

Greer knew that Janelle had spent a great deal of time preparing this case and was almost certain she would have won. Now, it looked as if all that time she'd put in had been wasted.

"Maybe they were holding one to his family," she countered, standing her ground against her indignant cousin.

The moment she made the suggestion, Greer could see that the explanation was more than acceptable to Kincannon. But his opinion wasn't the one that counted here.

Greer shifted her eyes toward the chief, holding her breath. Waiting.

"Maybe," Brian allowed slowly. "Makes sense," he decided. The chief turned toward two of the officers he'd summoned. "Mahoney, Wong, find out the bailiff's address. See if there's anything going on at his house that shouldn't be."

"His name's Tim Kelly," Kincannon informed them to facilitate the search. "Human Resources can give you the rest of the information. Their office is located on the third floor. Three-seventeen," the judge added for good measure. He wanted to clear the young man, wanted it not to be Tim's fault. Otherwise, it would make him begin to doubt his own judgment, and that was a dark place he never wanted to revisit.

They had their instructions so the two officers took off.

Belatedly, Blake felt a surge of adrenaline kick in. He

needed to be doing something. Blake looked at Brian. "Is there anything I can do to help? To move things along?" he wanted to know.

"Unless you can pull a felon out of a hat, Judge, I'd say go home. You're free for the afternoon," Brian added. Kincannon looked at him in surprise, forcing Brian to state the obvious. "I'm afraid that court's adjourned for the day, Judge. Everyone's court," he clarified in case there was any question. "There're a lot of places Munro could hide and it's going to take a while to conduct a completely thorough search. The bastard's got to be here somewhere."

"Not necessarily." All eyes turned to Greer. "Think about it. The fake ambulance has clearance to be on the grounds—and to leave. What's to have stopped them from backing the vehicle up in front of one of the side exits? With all this commotion, even with all the backup you called in, the officers can't be everywhere at once." She spread her hands. "Munro ducks out where they're not."

It seemed like a very simple explanation—and very doable. Greer continued. "The fake paramedics come back, pushing a gurney with a wounded victim. They load it and the bailiff into the back of the vehicle." She snapped her fingers. "One, two, three, they're gone and we're still hunting for Munro."

Brian frowned. It made sense. And he didn't like it.

"Let's hope they're not as bright as you are." But even as he said it, it was obvious to those around him that the chief of detectives knew there was a good chance that Greer was right. He offered his niece a quick smile.

"Just glad you're on our side," he told her. Turning back to his men, he directed the new groups to fan out everywhere and double-check the locations, including the basement—just in case.

With everything being done that could be done, Blake decided that he might as well do as the chief advised and go home. But first, he needed to take care of a few things of his own.

Returning to the courtroom again, Blake went directly to his administrative assistant, an older woman who wore sensible shoes and nondescript suits that never called attention to her. To the casual observer, Edith Fields looked like the very prototype of what had once been referred to as a mere secretary. Edith was that and so much more.

The moment she saw him, the grandmother of six— two of whom she was raising herself—was on her feet. "Any news, Your Honor?" she wanted to know. Blake knew it had never pleased her that the wheels of justice ground slowly. She wanted every criminal to be thrown into jail quickly, and left there for the duration of a maximum sentence.

"We're being sent home, Edith."

The news was not received well. The woman looked down at the compact laptop that sat on her desk, opened and at the ready. She read one of the entries on the judge's heavy schedule. "I could reschedule the Brown case, Your Honor."

Left on his own, he would have said yes, but the day belonged to Chief Cavanaugh and the latter called the shots. Blake shook his head.

"No point. We need to clear out of the courthouse." He saw that Edith was far from jubilant about the turn of events. "Think of this as an enforced holiday. I'm sure Joe could use a hand with Emily and Ross," he said, mentioning the names of the two grandchildren who lived with Edith and her husband of forty-one years.

The woman had made it known more than once that she thought she was indispensable to his court. She sighed now, a child being sent to her room for no good reason. "If you say so, Your Honor."

"The chief of detectives says so, Edith," Blake corrected. He glanced over his shoulder. Just as he thought, the detective was still there, like a shadow he couldn't cast off without taking drastic measures. "If you feel uneasy about leaving the courthouse, Edith," he told the older woman, "I can have Detective O'Brien take you home."

Greer blinked. Had he just volunteered her services without consulting her? She wasn't part of his team, to be ordered about, she thought, irritated at his cavalier manner.

She was about to protest, but as it turned out, she didn't have to. His administrative assistant dismissed the offer with a haughty wave of her hand.

"I'm a big girl, Judge. I stopped being afraid of thugs like Munro when I was in grammar school. He doesn't scare me." Her things packed, Edith nodded at her employer. "See you in the morning, Judge."

Blake barely nodded. A moment earlier, he'd crossed to his desk and was about initiate the procedure that would power down his computer when the big, bold letters that were written across the monitor's screen caught his attention.

And then raised his ire.

When he made no answer in response to his assistant, a woman he obviously held in warm regard, Greer looked at the judge. She saw the angry look that had darkened his features.

Kincannon was a formidable-looking man, she couldn't help thinking. She definitely wouldn't have wanted to find herself on the receiving end of that look. But right now, she was more curious as to what had caused it. It couldn't be the ongoing situation because he seemed to have calmed down about that—unlike her.

Maybe, instead of throwing herself on top of Kincannon, the situation would have been better served if she'd had the wherewithal to tackle Munro and keep him from fleeing. Growing up with her brothers as playmates and partners in crime had taught her to be fearless, reckless and unafraid of pain if enduring pain resulted in achieving a desired outcome. In this case, it would have been preventing that poor excuse for a human being from making good his escape.

Greer took a second look at Kincannon's expression. Something was off.

"What's wrong?" she wanted to know. Not waiting for an answer, she rounded Kincannon's desk and came up next to him. Since he was staring at the computer screen, Greer looked at it, as well. For a second, the words seemed too absurd to be real.

And then they were all too real.

*Back off or you and your father are going to die. Slowly and painfully.*

She thought Kincannon was going to hurl the laptop across the room, but he restrained himself. She heard him mutter angrily, "Brazen son of a bitch."

There was no question that this had come from Munro. "Obviously, he believes in the family plan," she commented. The next moment, she was hurrying out of the courtroom again.

Turning away from the courtroom in an attempt to create a pocket of privacy, Blake quickly took out his cell phone and turned it on. One of his pet peeves was cell phones that rang during court, but right now he was glad he had forgotten to leave his cell phone in the top desk drawer in his chambers. It saved him precious seconds he didn't know if he could afford to waste. He was not about to continue underestimating Munro.

"C'mon, answer," he ordered, addressing a man who wasn't there. The message he'd left on the answering machine at home was just kicking in when he glanced toward the double doors in the rear and saw O'Brien coming back—and she had the chief with her. "Pick up, Dad," Blake instructed through clenched teeth. "Pick up!"

And then he heard the receiver being lifted on the other end.

*Thank God.*

"Bad day in court?" he heard his father ask. "The story's all over the TV," Alexander Kincannon, retired marine sergeant and practicing malcontent, grumbled. "It preempted my show. What the hell kind of security have you got down there? Can't even hang on to one skinny criminal?" he demanded.

Blake was not in the mood to get drawn into a lengthy discussion about how lax current law enforcement had gotten. He needed for his father to listen to him. "Dad, I don't want you answering the door."

He heard his father blow out an irritated breath. "What am I, twelve?"

For a second, Blake lost patience. "You're a hundred and seven, but I want you to make it to a hundred and eight, Dad. Don't answer the door, do I make myself clear?"

"Why?" the gravelly voice demanded, sounding significantly less combative than it had just a moment earlier.

Reaching the judge and able to make out what the person on the other end was asking, Brian raised his voice so that the judge could hear him over the loud voice on the cell phone. "Tell him I'm sending a patrol car over. It'll be there in a few minutes." He made eye contact with Kincannon. "We'll keep him safe."

Blake nodded his thanks toward the chief. "Dad, they're sending a—"

"I heard, I heard." Alexander cut him off. "I'm not deaf yet, you know." And then a degree of excitement entered his voice. "This have anything to do with that pusher who took a powder?"

"Maybe. I don't know yet." Although, he added silently, he was pretty certain that it was. Blake heard his father sigh dramatically and then abruptly terminate the connection. Closing his own phone, Blake slipped it back into the pocket of his robe. He looked at Brian, his gratitude rising to the foreground. "Thank you."

"Least I can do," Brian acknowledged, then he nodded toward his niece. "Greer alerted me to the message you received on your laptop." He lowered his eyes to the state-of-the-art computer on the judge's desk. "I'm going to have to take it, Your Honor. Maybe one of our people can trace where the e-mail originated." He knew for a fact that Brenda, his son Dax's wife, would all but make a computer sit up and beg. Maybe she could pull this miracle off, as well.

Ordinarily, Blake might have protested about protecting the privacy of his court cases, but in this case, there was no need. Brian Cavanaugh was a veritable pillar of ethics. So he nodded, turning the laptop around and handing it over to the chief.

"Whatever you need," he told the older man.

Brian closed the lid, securing it in place. "Right now, it's what you need that's important," he corrected. "It looks as if this Munro character feels he has a specific beef with you that goes beyond his own case. As I heard it, you sent several of his people away with the maximum sentence when they were convicted a couple of years ago."

Blake wanted no credit for serving justice. It was what it was. "Just doing my job, Chief."

"And now I'm doing mine," Brian countered. "You need protection, Judge."

Blake did not savor relinquishing his privacy, but there was his father to think of, so he nodded.

"A patrol car making the rounds every hour or so should do it," he speculated.

"What about the other fifty-nine minutes?" Brian asked mildly.

Blake's eyes narrowed as he tried to follow the chief's reasoning. "Excuse me?"

"The way I see it, Judge, until this drug dealer is caught, you're going to need twenty-four-hour protection, not just a patrol car passing by every now and then."

Blake didn't want to argue, but he definitely didn't want to acquiesce, either. "Isn't that a little extreme, Chief?"

"Death is extreme, Judge, everything else is a distant second," Greer pointed out, feeling that the chief could use a little verbal backup right about now. She could understand the desire to remain independent. In the judge's place, she'd feel the same way. But Munro would think nothing of putting a bullet right between the judge's eyes. It would seem like a crime to disfigure that noble profile with a bullet.

In return for her support, Greer saw the chief smile at her. She returned the smile, not recognizing the expression for what it was. Had she been part of the family longer, she might have known that the smile that was curving his mouth was the one Brian wore when he was about to deliver a very salient point, and triumphantly drive it home.

"I'm glad you feel that way, Greer."

She might not have been able to pick up on the chief's expressions, but there was something in his tone of voice that softly warned her she was in big trouble. Not the disciplinary kind, but the kind that meant she was on the verge of something she would regard as less than pleasant happening.

"Why, sir?" she asked her superior quietly, never taking her eyes off Brian's face.

Even as Greer asked for clarification, she had a sinking feeling in the pit of her stomach that she knew why Brian had just expressed his satisfaction at her agreement.

"Because I'm assigning you to be Judge Kincannon's bodyguard."

It was hard to say which of them was more averse to the news they'd just received, she or Kincannon.

"I'm not going into hiding," Blake protested with feeling.

"Nobody said anything about hiding," Brian told him. With enough effort, they could keep the judge safe and still presiding over his courtroom. But it would be tricky. Which was why he felt that Greer was the person for the job. She was a self-starter who thought outside the box.

"Look, Chief Cavanaugh," Blake began again, picking his words slowly, "I'm very grateful that you're sending a car to watch over my father, but I'm not a helpless old man—"

He could just hear his father's reaction to that description. At seventy-three, the former gunnery sergeant was still fit, still capable of pummeling someone to the ground with his fists as long as that someone didn't tower more than six inches over him. There was nothing "ex" about this marine.

"A bullet is a great equalizer."

Had that come out of her mouth? Greer thought suddenly. Even suppressing annoyance at the confining assignment she'd just been handed, she found herself still performing like a good little soldier. Pressing her lips together, she caught herself longing for the days that she'd been a rebel. A rebel wasn't in danger of going comatose standing guard over someone. Being a bodyguard was only marginally better than being forced to sit in a car, maintaining surveillance on a suspect. She hated both assignments with a passion. Inactivity was not in her DNA.

But it looked like, judging by the chief's expression, she was stuck.

Maybe so, she thought the next moment, but she wasn't about to go down without a fight—or without going on record that she was less than thrilled with the assignment.

"That's right, it is," Brian agreed with Greer's succinct assessment. He smiled at his niece, clearly appreciating the backup. "Now," the chief continued, "until we finally catch this Munro character, you're assigned to the judge."

Finally. She didn't know if she had as much faith in the wheels of justice as he apparently did. Finally could mean days, or, more likely, it could mean weeks. She didn't want to spend weeks babysitting, even if the person she was watching over was an incredibly good-looking specimen of manhood.

She was a good detective. She belonged in the

field, damn it, not hovering over the judge like some misguided shadow.

"Chief, could I have a word with you?" she requested as he began to walk away.

Rather than answer verbally, Brian beckoned her to follow him as he walked out of the courtroom. With the judge's laptop tucked under his arm.

## Chapter 4

Greer stared at the chief of detectives' back as she followed him into the hallway. Considering the stress and pressure he was always under, the man exuded strength and energy.

There was a lot to live up to being a Cavanaugh, she thought. People expected you to be at the top of your game, sharp and in good physical condition at the same time. It just went with the territory.

For the most part, the commotion in the hallway had died down. The area was relatively empty now. People had been taken aside for questioning and the rest of the police who'd been summoned were scattered throughout the building, conducting an intense room-to-room search.

But her mind wasn't on the hallway or what was happening beyond it. Greer's mind was on what she was going to say to the chief and how she was going to say it in order to hopefully get him to see things her way.

She *really* didn't want to take on this assignment and her primary reason didn't even have anything to do with her staunch dislike of inactivity. It went far deeper than that.

It was times like these that she really wished she had Ethan's golden tongue and his effortless ability to phrase things just right. But she didn't. All she could do was state her case as best as possible and cross her fingers that it was good enough. Cross her fingers that the chief would understand and see things from her point of view.

Putting her request in the form of a plea wouldn't carry any weight, she knew that. Even if it did, she didn't think she was capable of resorting to begging. Begging wasn't in her inherent makeup. She'd always taken her medicine and stoically faced up to her responsibilities, no matter what.

But in this case, it wasn't just that *she* didn't want to have to be the judge's bodyguard. She was more than fairly certain that Kincannon wouldn't want her hovering around him 24/7, or whatever ratio of time the chief decided that she had to put in. If the judge was forced to put up with a bodyguard—and from where she stood, she could see why it would be necessary—she was sure that she wouldn't be the man's first choice. Not by a long shot.

Brian abruptly stopped several feet beyond the courtroom's double doors. Preoccupied, searching for the proper wording, Greer almost walked right into him. Catching herself, she stopped approximately an inch shy of colliding with her superior.

Sucking in her breath, she quickly backed up so that there was a decent amount of space between them. Under no circumstances did she want to appear to be crowding the man.

"Now, what is it you want to talk to me about?" Brian asked her genially.

By his tone and expression, the topic of conversation could have involved something personal and inconsequential. But Greer kept her guard up. He might be her uncle, but here, on the job, he was the man who was ultimately in charge. Family ties didn't enter into it.

She reminded herself that, like the judge, Brian was tough, but fair. At best, she had a fifty-fifty chance. She'd had worse odds.

Greer forged ahead. "With all due respect, Chief, I'd rather you assigned someone else to be the judge's bodyguard."

"And why is that?" he asked her, his voice mild.

She cleared her throat, trying her best not to make this sound as if she was asking for preferential treatment, because she wasn't.

"The judge and I…" She stumbled, then tried again. "We have some history."

His expression never changed. "Were you lovers?"

Some of the air seemed to vanish from her lungs. Her eyes widened in disbelief. "No! No," she repeated, doing her best to sound calm this time. "I… That is, he…"

It was not in his nature to make his people uncomfortable. That went double for family. Brian raised his hand, interrupting the halting flow of words. "If you're about to refer to what I think you're going to refer to, I'm well aware of your 'history' with the judge, Greer," he told her.

She stared at him, stunned and at the same time, relieved that she wasn't going to have to relive the ordeal by rendering a blow-by-blow description for him. "You are?"

The nod was almost imperceptible. "I made it a point to familiarize myself with your files—yours and your brothers'," he clarified, not wanting her to think that he had singled her out for some reason. She was fairly new in this position and second-guessing was part of the process. He didn't want to add a strong case of paranoia. "I like to know things about my family—and the people who ultimately work under me," he explained, answering questions he knew she had to be thinking.

Greer took a breath. This had been easier than she thought. "So then you understand why I think it would be better if someone else was assigned to the judge?"

"No."

The one word answer came out of nowhere and hit her like a detonating bomb. "No?" she echoed, hoping she'd heard wrong.

"No," Brian repeated. His tone was mild, but there was no mistaking the firm undertone. "You are the most qualified to handle the job right now. You know the judge and, more importantly, you're familiar with Munro, with the way he thinks, the way he acts." That, he indicated, was of paramount importance. "That puts you several steps ahead of anyone else I'd assign to the detail," he told her. "It only makes sense that I put you in charge."

It might make sense to him, she thought, but that still didn't make her comfortable with it. "Chief." The single word packed all the appeal into it that she could muster.

The chief looked at her for a long moment, his gaze drying up whatever words she was planning to use. Drying up the words and her saliva, as well. It felt as if she had a mouthful of sand.

"You're not asking me to give you special consideration, are you, Greer?" he finally asked.

God, she didn't want him to think that. She shook her head with feeling. His tone had been low. Hers wasn't. "No, sir."

Brian's smile was easy, pleasant. "Good, I didn't think so." About to turn away, he realized that he hadn't finished yet. "How long will it take you to go home and pack some things?"

Somewhere distant in her head, she heard a door slamming. The door had bars on it. She was stuck. She was just going to have to make the best of it. "I've got a change of clothes in the car."

The information had Brian's smile widening. "You're a Cavanaugh, all right. Always prepared."

His compliment reminded her of something. Greer shifted slightly. "About that, sir?" she began, letting her voice trail off a little.

Brian waited.

There were seven of them, seven "new" members

of the family. There were the four who belonged to his bride of a little more than a year, and then there were the three who none of them had been prepared for. Triplets who comprised his late brother Mike's secret other family. Lila's children, all adults and all on the force, went by her first husband's surname while Greer and her brothers had her late mother's. All seven were told that they were welcomed to change their names to Cavanaugh if they wanted to.

Name change or not, that was what they were. Cavanaughs. But the decision strictly belonged to the seven individuals involved. He'd heard that it was going to be an "all-or-nothing" deal. The "jury" was still out on which way they would ultimately lean.

Or maybe the jury was ready to come in, he thought, looking down at the young woman who reminded him so much of Mike's daughter, Patience.

"Yes?" he prodded.

She pressed her lips together. "For my part, I've decided yes."

"Yes?" he echoed, unclear if it was "yes" she'd change her surname to Cavanaugh or "yes," she'd keep the one she already had.

"Yes," she repeated. "If it were only up to me, I'd like to change my last name to Cavanaugh. It'd be an honor."

"We'd all like that," he assured her. "Especially Andrew. And the honor goes both ways," he added. "Anything else?"

"No, sir, that's all." Finished, Greer began to back up, trying not to dread what lay ahead. She was fairly certain that the judge wouldn't bring up their first encounter, he seemed too self-contained for that, but she was fairly sure that the memory was probably never far from his mind. Which would make things very awkward and difficult between them.

Nobody said being a cop was going to be easy, she reminded herself.

"Good," Brian was saying. "Then go tell the judge that you're going to be his new houseguest for the foreseeable future."

Nodding, Greer drew in a deep, fortifying breath. There was no way around this.

Who knew, maybe they'd get lucky and one of the chief's men had already located Munro at the bailiff's house.

Greer had her doubts but she mentally crossed her fingers anyway as she turned around and pushed open the padded black leather doors. For what felt like the umpteenth time that day, she walked into the courtroom.

The judge wasn't there.

Adrenaline shot through her veins like a spring-propelled pinball. Greer quickly scanned the room. There was no sign of the man she was supposed to be guarding. The only one left in the room was the court stenographer, carefully packing up her steno machine.

Greer hurried over to the thin blonde. "Where's the judge?" she demanded.

Closing the case and snapping its locks into place, the woman picked up her equipment. She made no secret of the fact that she was eager to leave. The unexpected question made her frown thoughtfully.

"In his chambers, I guess," she replied.

"I hope you guessed right," Greer muttered under her breath as she hurried to the rear of the room. There was an exit to the right of the judge's desk. This had to be what he'd used to pull his disappearing act.

Damn it, she thought, finding herself in a narrow hallway, why couldn't the man stay put? Didn't he understand the gravity of the situation? Or did Kincannon understand it and just believed himself to be bulletproof?

Turning a corner, she found herself facing a closed door. She had her weapon out and ready to fire in one swift movement. There was no telling what she'd find on the other side of the door. For all she knew, Munro had been lying in wait for the judge in his own chambers. The drug dealer was just crazy enough to do it.

Biting off a few choice words, she kicked open the door, weapon aimed and poised to shoot at anything that made a wrong move.

Startled, the man inside the room swung around.

Kincannon.

Alone.

A hiss of air escaped through her clenched teeth and Greer lowered her weapon. Relief and anger converged within her.

Before she'd made her entrance, the judge had taken off his robe and hung it carefully on a hanger, apparently respectful of all the black cloth represented. He frowned now as she lowered her weapon.

"Most people knock before kicking down a door and bursting into someone's chambers." His voice was deceptively calm.

Greer's mouth dropped open. He was going to be high-handed and lecture her? Seriously? "First of all, I didn't kick down the door. It's still attached."

"The maintenance man will be grateful," he commented drolly.

"And second," she continued, pretending he hadn't said anything, "most people don't have an escaped felon threatening to kill them. Drastic times require drastic measures." Her look pinned him where he stood. "You shouldn't have wandered off like that."

"I'm a grown man and in possession of all my faculties," he told her tersely. "I didn't 'wander off,' I went to my chambers. For a reason," he added.

"To hang up your robe?" Greer guessed incredulously.

"Yes." He said the single word as if it was a challenge.

She was not about to back off. If this was going to work between them, he had to be aware of the rules. "You could have waited."

"I could have," he agreed. "But I didn't. Detective, I've been crossing the street by myself since I was six years old. Nothing's happened yet." He blew out a breath, as if he was trying to calm himself. "And in case you're interested, this isn't the first threat I've gotten," he assured her.

"It's the first on my watch," she informed him. And then she asked the question that was nagging at her.

"Since you were six? Seriously?" Who let their six-year-old cross the street by themselves?

"My father insisted. He wouldn't let my mother coddle me. Said it was important for me to become a man."

"At six?" she cried. "How many six-year-old men did he know?"

He'd never questioned his father's reasons or methods. That was just the way things were. "He was a marine, a gunnery sergeant in the corps."

The light began to seep in, shining on the situation. "That explains a lot."

He disregarded her comment. "What are you doing here, Detective? I assumed you weren't going to be 'watching over' me anymore. Isn't that what you wanted to tell the chief? That you'd rather pass on the assignment?"

They were back to awkward again, she thought. She didn't like him just "assuming" things about her—even if they were true. "The chief would rather that I didn't 'pass.'"

He looked at her, vindicated. Up until this moment, he'd just been guessing, but her admission had just proven him right. "Then you did protest."

She raised her chin. If she was going to have to do this, it was best if there were no hard feelings between them. "*Protest* is rather a strong word, Judge."

He laughed shortly. "Don't split hairs, Detective O'Brien. It's not your style."

Now he was assuming things about her? She didn't

care for being pigeonholed. "And how would you know what my 'style' was?"

The answer to that was far less complex than she might assume, Blake thought. "I'm the man you jumped on, remember?" He saw what he took to be a slight blush accent her cheeks and found himself momentarily intrigued. He hadn't thought that they made women who blushed anymore. "You're given to broad strokes," he continued with his analysis, "not tiny lines."

She had always been a big picture kind of person. It made taking care of details particularly difficult for her. There was always something that she missed, that she forgot. Right now, the fact that Kincannon had nailed her so accurately made her very uncomfortable. Made her feel as if he was poking around in her head, invading her space.

She resented it. This wasn't going to work. And while she wasn't about to go back to the chief with that— Kincannon could.

"If you'd rather have someone else assigned to you, Your Honor, please feel free to ask the chief," she told him. "I'm sure he'd listen to you."

"I'd rather that no one was assigned to me," he told her curtly, "but you saw where that went."

Tired of dancing around in circles, she shrugged off the whole situation. "Maybe you'll get lucky and the chief's men'll find Munro quickly."

Blake sincerely doubted that luck was on his side. Munro had probably gone underground. "Lots of places a man can disappear in this county." He looked at her pointedly. "Or out of it. If Munro had any brains at all, he's take this opportunity to flee the country—at least until things cool off for him."

"Oh, he has brains all right," Greer assured him. She'd dealt with people like Munro before, too often for her liking. In her opinion, they were the vermin of the earth. But Munro seemed to be a cut above the rest. Smarter. Sharper. And that worried her as far as the judge's safety went. "But he's also the type who relishes taking revenge."

Taking his jacket out of the small closet, Blake slipped it on over his light blue tapered shirt. "In that case, shouldn't you be the one with a bodyguard?" he asked. "After all, you were the one who pulled off that sting and brought Munro in."

"But you were the judge who sent away his buddies," she reminded him. And there was one more salient point. "And you were the one who got the e-mail."

To her surprise, just the barest hint of a smile curved the corners of a mouth that could have been called sensual under different circumstances. He shrugged at her words. "It was worth a shot."

Swiftly, she pieced things together. "You were trying to talk me out of guarding you?"

It was obvious that the man she was going to be protecting saw no reason to offer a denial. "I was."

Well, he'd wasted his time, she thought. "It's not up to me."

"And if it was up to you?" he wanted to know. "Would you guard me?"

She could smell the lather he'd used shaving. Or maybe that was the scent of his soap. In any case, he was standing too close, she thought. His space was commingling with hers and that was definitely interfering with her thought process.

Greer subtly moved over to where his robe was hanging and pretended to be interested in the texture of the weave. It was called survival.

The automatic response to his question would have been no. But this didn't require an automatic answer, it required one that had some thought behind it. The chief never said things just to hear himself talk. If he felt the judge needed a bodyguard, then he damn well needed a bodyguard. She'd already silently agreed with that judgment.

She worded her response carefully. "If there was no one else to do it, yes, I would."

His eyes held hers for a moment. She felt as if he was looking into her soul. "A truthful answer."

There was a reason for that. The judge wasn't the kind of man you lied to. Not without a great many consequences. "I've got a feeling you could see right through it if it wasn't."

Her answer amused him. Was she applying the catch-more-flies-with-honey-than-with-vinegar theory? "Flattery, Detective?"

Her answer was immediate. "Observation, Judge." She glanced at what he was doing. Briefcase packed, he was apparently ready to go. Striding, he got ahead of her by the time they reached the door.

"My car's parked downstairs," he told her, leading the way out. Devoid of people, the courtroom was as quiet as a tomb. Alert, she scanned the area as she took the lead, not letting him walk until she walked there first.

"We'll take mine," she informed him. There was no room for argument.

He did anyway. "I'm partial to my car." Reaching the elevators, he pressed the down button.

"And I'm partial to you breathing," she replied mildly.

The wording surprised him. "Really?"

"Okay," she admitted, "the chief is. And what the chief wants, the chief gets."

She was overreacting, he thought. He refused to be intimated by a cheap hood.

"And you really think that if I use my car, I won't be 'breathing' for much longer?" He didn't bother removing the note of mockery in his voice. "Just how much credit are you giving this two-bit criminal?"

The elevator arrived. She held her hand up, stopping the judge until she checked out the interior. There were two other people in the car, both wearing ID badges that connected them to Human Resources.

She motioned him forward with the barrel of her weapon. "The kind of credit that goes along with having a bogus paramedic team arrive on the scene well ahead of the real one. The kind of credit someone who could pull this all off should be awarded. Anything else?" she wanted to know.

"Yes. Are you always this annoying?"

The question caught her off guard, although she didn't show it.

"No," Greer finally replied. "If you believe my

brothers, sometimes I'm worse." The doors opened on the first floor. She waited for the two people to disembark, then motioned for the judge to follow her. "Let's go, Your Honor."

Rather than follow, he fell into step beside her even as he resigned himself to the inevitable. "I have no choice, I guess."

"Nope."

They made their way to the front doors. There were several police officers, all of whom she was familiar with, processing people out one by one. Recognizing them, one of the officers waved her and the judge by.

Greer stopped just before the doors and her eyes met Kincannon's. "Neither one of us do."

And, she had a strong feeling as they exited, neither one of them was very happy about this state of affairs, either.

# Chapter 5

"So how is this going to work?" the judge asked her once they were in her car and she was pulling out of the parking structure. "Do I check with you before I take a breath?"

Greer kept her eyes on the road as she exited onto the street. She supposed she could understand his sarcasm. In Kincannon's place, she'd probably feel the same way.

No, she corrected herself, not probably, she would *definitely* feel the same way. She'd never liked restrictions and living with a bodyguard was the very definition of being restricted. But then, he'd chosen this career. No one had forced it on him.

"No," she replied mildly, acting as if he'd just asked her a legitimate question, "how many breaths you take or don't take is entirely up to you."

She heard him sigh. A glance in his direction told her he was staring out the windshield and frowning.

"You know this is completely unnecessary, don't you?" he said.

Anyone who could orchestrate a successful escape from a courtroom was a man to be reckoned with—and not underestimated. If Munro wanted to enact his revenge against the judge, then the judge needed serious protection.

"Sorry, Your Honor," she answered, "but I don't know anything of the kind."

"I know how to defend myself, Detective O'Brien," he informed her, his impatience barely contained.

She pretended she didn't hear the annoyance in his voice. "Good, then this shouldn't be a difficult assignment for me."

He tried again. He knew she was only doing her job, but there was no point in doing it with him. "My father was a marine."

*At least you knew your father.* Sparing him another glance, she forced a smile to her lips. "So you said. And I'm sure he was an excellent one."

It didn't end there. "The point of my reference," he told her caustically, "is that he insisted on teaching me self-defense."

She eased her vehicle into a right turn. She had a tendency to turn sharply and she didn't want him complaining that her driving was making him ill on top of everything else.

"Did he also teach you how to catch bullets with your bare hands?" she asked mildly.

"No."

She nodded at his reply. "Then I'm afraid you need me."

"Why?" he wanted to know. "Do you catch bullets with your bare hands?"

"No, but I have a gun—" Greer began. She no longer thought of him as the man whose wife she couldn't save. She was now beginning to regard him as a judge who was a pain in her anatomy.

"So do I," he cut in.

Greer was tempted to pull over, but the sooner she got him home, the sooner they would be out of this confining space.

She sighed. "Judge, this is going to go a whole lot easier for both of us if you stop fighting the inevitable." Stepping on the gas, she just made it through a yellow light. "I've been assigned to you and I'm not leaving until either Eddie Munro is caught or the chief decides to replace me, so you might as well make the best of it." She deliberately kept her eyes forward. "I promise I'll try to be as unobtrusive as possible. You'll hardly notice I'm there."

There was silence for a moment. Had she won? Greer slanted a look in Kincannon's direction and instantly became aware of Kincannon's eyes moving over her slowly, as if to take measure of every inch of her. More criticism was coming, she could feel it.

"Oh," the judge replied, "I sincerely doubt that."

The comment took her completely by surprise. As did the unexpected and sudden feeling of warmth that was spreading throughout her torso and limbs. The same kind of warmth that had zapped through her when she'd thrown herself on top of the judge to shield him earlier.

At the time she'd attributed the reaction to adrenaline and the sudden, gut-seizing fear that she might not get Kincannon out of the line of fire in time. This time there was no one pointing a gun, no visible threat at all.

There was just the judge, appraising her. And obviously seeing her as a woman.

Greer cleared her throat, searching for something to fill the uncomfortable silence. "I heard you mention that your father's living with you."

His living arrangements were no secret. After the accident that had claimed his wife, his father had come from Maryland to lend him moral support. Initially, he'd been in an emotional tailspin, one that, at the time, it didn't seem possible he would ever get out of. But eventually he did. His father stayed on. A month turned into two years. Enamored with the weather, his father showed no signs of wanting to leave. And although the man was rather difficult and cantankerous at times, Blake had to admit that he enjoyed having someone to come home to.

"He is," the judge replied, wondering where this was going.

From what she'd picked up, the senior Kincannon was not that keen on women in the services. She imagined that extended to having women on the police force. "Do you think he'll be upset?"

"What, that he didn't get his own bodyguard?" the judge guessed at her meaning and recalled his phone call to his father. "My father would be insulted if it was even suggested."

She shook her head as she took another slow right turn. "No, I mean with my having to remain on the premises for a while. If he's old school—"

That was the polite way to describe it. Chauvinistic could be another. "He is."

There was only one conclusion to be drawn from that. "Then this might not sit too well with him."

For the first time, Blake smiled and Greer caught herself noticing how his features instantly softened. He even looked somewhat boyish. That definitely wasn't the impression she had when Kincannon wasn't smiling. Then he looked strict and stern, like a man who was not to be crossed.

"No," he agreed. "You're right. It might not. I'd brace myself if I were you, Detective." But even as he said it, his smile widened. "It just might turn out to be one hell of a bumpy ride."

He probably thought that would make her ask to be taken off the assignment. *You don't know me, Judge.* "I've had bumpy rides before."

Kincannon didn't offer an argument, just a smile, a different kind this time. One that said he had some sort of inside knowledge that she wasn't privy to—yet. But she would. It was just a matter of time.

"We'll see, Detective," he said, an ominous promise in his voice. "We'll see."

"What are you doing home so early?" were Alexander Kincannon's first words to his son when Blake walked into his two-story house fifteen minutes later.

Before Blake could say anything in response, Greer walked in behind him. The senior Kincannon, who was nearly as tall as his son and seemed to have a good twenty, thirty pounds on him, grinned knowingly.

"Oh, I see. Looks like I got my answer." The words were directed at his son, but the ex-marine made absolutely no secret of the fact that he was staring at the woman beside Blake. The older man circled her as if to get the full effect. "Good to see you dating again, Blake. About time, too." And then his grin became positively wicked. "Did you bring one for me?"

Blake glanced at his watch. It had taken his father all of thirty seconds to embarrass him.

"I'm not 'dating again,' Dad," he answered, doing his best to remain patient with the man. He had no desire to lose his temper with his father in front of a stranger. For the most part, he was a private person. Far more private, apparently, than his father.

"Then who's this?" Alexander wanted to know.

"'This,'" Blake answered, using his father's exact phrasing, "is Detective Greer O'Brien." He paused for a moment before adding, "Our bodyguard."

Sky-blue eyes beneath bushy gray eyebrows that resembled miniature tumbleweeds widened incredulously. "Bodyguard?" the ex-marine hooted. His message was clear. The practical joke that his son was obviously attempting to play had just fallen flat. "Yeah, right." He turned toward the woman. His expression told her that he liked what he saw. "Who are you, really, honey?"

Honey. Greer knew she should have been offended to

be addressed that way, but she had a feeling that the older man didn't mean anything by it. In his generation, it was perfectly acceptable to address a young female that way. In a way, his manner was almost oddly endearing.

Maybe, she thought, because in a way, Kincannon's father reminded her of her grandfather. Her mother's father had been one of those grumpy old men with a heart of gold who existed in sitcoms and other people's family trees. He had been in hers and she'd loved him dearly—they all had—from the moment she'd known him until the day he died. She was ten at the time and completely devastated over the loss.

"Exactly who your son says I am," she told him. "Detective Greer O'Brien." Greer put her hand out to the senior Kincannon. "I've been assigned to keep you and your son safe and out of harm's way."

Alexander eyed her hand without taking it. "And who's going to keep you safe and out of harm's way?" he asked gruffly.

Greer never hesitated. "You, sir. We can watch each other's backs."

The answer couldn't have pleased Alexander more. He nodded his full head of silver-gray hair as he took the hand she was still offering. He shook it firmly and noted that she returned the handshake in kind. "I was a marine, you know."

The look in the man's eyes told Greer that she'd scored points. "I could tell by your bearing, sir. Once a marine, always a marine."

"You bet your a—backside," Alexander concluded,

stopping himself at the last minute from saying the word he ordinarily used.

Greer grinned, silently telegraphing that she appreciated the courtesy.

Releasing her hand, Alexander looked at his son. "So, aside from getting shot at, losing a prisoner and gaining a bodyguard with killer legs, how did the rest of your day go?" he asked.

"That about covers the highlights," Blake replied. Shedding his jacket and tie, the judge left them slung over the back of the first chair he came to on his way to the liquor cabinet.

When he took out a decanter of scotch, Greer tactfully suggested, "Shouldn't you have something to eat, first?"

Suppressing an irritated sigh, Blake glanced at her over his shoulder. "Detective, you were assigned to be my bodyguard, right?"

"Right."

He placed the decanter on the counter. "Unless I'm mistaken, that means you're supposed to guard the outside of my body, not the inside."

He was going to fight her all the way, wasn't he? No matter what she said. Well, she didn't join the force expecting it to be a piece of cake.

Greer crossed to him. "Having something in your stomach reduces the effects of the alcohol. I just wanted to make things easier on you."

His eyes met hers. His were a piercing blue, a shade darker than his father's, she noted. "What would accomplish that is if you folded your tent and disappeared into the night."

She refused to rise to the bait. Instead, she smiled brightly. She had a hunch that it drove him crazy. "Night doesn't come for several hours yet, Your Honor," she informed him.

"Is that when you leave?" Alexander asked, joining her.

"No." As far as she knew, there weren't going to be shifts. There was just going to be her. She had a feeling, though, as the assignment stretched out, adjustments would be made. "That's just when the judge would want me to leave."

Alexander snorted dismissively as he waved a hand in his son's direction. "Don't pay any attention to him. Outside the courtroom, Blake doesn't have the sense he was born with."

"I'm standing right here, Dad," Blake pointed out, raising his voice.

Alexander spared his son a withering glance. "You're six foot two, boy, and my vision's still good. I can see you."

"Then don't talk about me as if I'm not in the room," Blake suggested.

"Even when you are, half the time you're not." Alexander looked back at Greer and confided in a voice that had never quite dipped down to the level of a whisper, "His mind wanders worse than an old man's. Not that I'd know anything about that." He chuckled.

Greer nodded. "Didn't think you would. Mr.

Kincannon—" she began, only to have the senior Kincannon interrupt.

"Gunny," he told her. "Call me Gunny. I was a gunnery sergeant in the marines."

She inclined her head, wordlessly thanking the older man for the privilege of calling him by the common nickname awarded to all those who served as gunnery sergeants in the corps.

"Gunny," she echoed. "Could I ask you to show me around your house?"

The older man beamed, then cleared his throat as he went through the motions of summoning a sterner look. "I suppose I can find time for that."

The corners of her mouth curved. "I'd appreciate it, Gunny."

Squaring his shoulders, the still exceedingly robust retired marine began leading her to the next room. "Okay, that was the living room. Over here you've got your..."

As his father's voice faded away, taking his unwanted houseguest with him, Blake could only shake his head. He was far from happy about this unexpected turn of events. He hadn't lied to Detective O'Brien just to make her back off. He had been threatened before, threatened verbally with physical harm, he'd just never told anyone. And, because he'd never registered a complaint with the police, his life had remained his own.

Moreover, no one had come to shoot him dead. The threats had remained empty.

As empty as this one probably was. The only difference was that this time, the threat had been witnessed, so to speak, by the chief of detectives. That had made it official and there was no getting around the rules.

That didn't mean he had to like it. Or even think that the slip of a woman the chief had assigned to him would make a difference. If that despicable excuse for a human being, Munro, wanted to do away with him, Blake knew that, bodyguard or no bodyguard, the drug dealer was damn well going to try to kill him.

However, he liked to think that he was at least smarter than a hood like Munro no matter how much money the drug dealer had tucked away in a Cayman Islands bank account. And he didn't want the likes of Detective O'Brien getting in the way and possibly getting caught in the ensuing cross fire.

He didn't need her on his conscience. He already had Margaret.

Blake poured himself two fingers worth of scotch and brought the glass to his lips. He was about to take a hearty swallow when he stopped and then set the glass back down on the counter. With a sigh, he looked down and contemplated the contents he'd just poured.

Drinking wasn't going to make the situation *or* the detective go away and it just might have an unwanted effect his judgment. With another sigh, Blake took the glass and ever so slowly poured the amber liquid back onto the decanter.

He'd just put the stopper back into the mouth of the bottle when he heard his father's voice. It sounded as if the man was getting closer. The unnerving thing was that it was unusually jovial—for his father.

At least this detective had done one thing, he thought.

She'd managed to tame the savage beast that beat within his father's chest.

The woman, he mused, apparently had some hidden talents.

Walking into the family room, Greer glanced at the glass on top of the small bar and immediately noted that it was empty.

"Finished your drink so soon?" his father asked. There was a touch of admiration in his voice. "Didn't realize you could pack 'em away so fast, son."

"A lot of things you didn't realize," Blake replied mildly.

He was caught off guard when his so-called bodyguard not only came closer, she invaded his personal space. Glancing back at her guide, she said, "Your son didn't have a drink."

Blake said nothing, but their eyes met and held for a long moment, as if he expected her to follow up her theory with hard evidence.

His father picked up the glass from the counter. "Glass is coated."

"He poured it back into the decanter," Greer told him.

Okay, he wanted to know how she'd pulled off this parlor trick.

"And how would you know that?" Blake asked.

"Easy. You would have had to down the drink quickly and your breath would have reflected your consumption," she explained diplomatically. "There is no scotch on your breath. And the sides of the decanter have a little bit of an amber coating to them."

"Forensics 101?" Blake asked in a mocking tone.

Greer shook her head. "No, Agatha Christie. Miss Marple," she added, naming one of the famed mystery writer's more famous characters. "I forget which one of her books."

She heard Kincannon's father chuckling behind her. At least she'd won one of them over, Greer thought.

## Chapter 6

Greer spent the next couple of hours going over every inch of the first floor of the house, inside and out, securing it wherever necessary so that the front door was the only way for anyone to enter or exit.

The judge had a security system which she reprogrammed after advising him of the change and the new code. She did it just in case someone at the security company's home base had hacked into the system and acquired what was now the old code. Changing it, she'd told the judge, was going to be an ongoing daily proposition until the threat was over.

Kincannon hadn't looked overly happy about the idea of having to remember a new pass code every day, but at least he hadn't offered any resistance. He seemed far more interested in having her leave his office so he could get back to working on whatever it was that had claimed his attention.

She staked out the sofa, intending to spend the night on it. From there, she had a clear view of the door. Since she was an incredibly light sleeper to begin with, she had no doubt that any intruder attempting to enter the house would have her awake and on her feet in a matter of seconds.

Finished with her preparations for now, she walked back into the living room only to have Alexander ask her, "What'll you have, pizza or Chinese?"

Greer stared at the barrel-chested man, caught off guard by his question. "Excuse me?"

He raised the telephone receiver he was holding in the air as if to clarify that he was about to order in. "Food. So what'll it be?"

"You don't have to go to any special trouble for me," Greer protested.

"This isn't special," he informed her. "This is what we do every night."

Her eyes narrowed as the meaning of his words sank in. "You order in every night?"

"It's either that, or starve," the retired marine told her.

She shuddered to think what ingesting processed foods every night had to be doing to their digestive tracts. But then, maybe the old man was just exaggerating. "You don't have any food in your refrigerator?"

"Sure we've got food," he informed her matter-of-factly. "Leftovers."

"From the takeout," she guessed. Alexander nodded

his head. Didn't either of them have any idea about the value of proper nutrition?

"Well, yeah, sure," Gunny replied as if the answer was a no-brainer.

Very politely, she removed the receiver from his hand and replaced it in the cradle. "How long has it been since you had a home-cooked meal, Gunny?"

The senior Kincannon paused to think. And then he smiled as the memory obviously came back to him. "Well, there was that cute little Fraulein in Berlin... But that was about two years ago."

"You're kidding, right?" Greer said incredulously.

"Why would he kid about something like that?" Blake asked. Drawn by the voices, he walked into the room. Now what was this woman up to?

Greer shifted in order to look at both Kincannon men. "Let me get this straight, neither one of you has had a home-cooked meal in two years?" She stressed the last two words.

"You deaf, girl?" Alexander asked impatiently. He began to reach for the phone again, but she rested her hand on the receiver, immobilizing it.

"No, but I am stunned," Greer admitted.

"What's the big deal?" Alexander wanted to know. "It's all just fuel and it all turns into the same thing on its way out."

"Colorful," Greer commented. "Be that as it may," she continued, "you're not doing yourselves any favors with all that takeout food."

Curious and wanting to see for herself, Greer passed the judge's father and went into the kitchen. She opened the refrigerator. There were several bottles of beer, domestic and imported, a partial loaf of white bread, the wrapper only loosely tied and most likely harboring stale slices, and a lone stick of butter.

"You weren't kidding," she murmured under her breath as she shook her head.

"So, what'll it be?" Alexander repeated, on his way back to the landline. "Pizza or Chinese?"

"Hang on a minute," she called out. Crossing back to the living room, she took out her cell phone and went through the directory. She found the number she was looking for and pressed the buttons that would connect her. As the phone rang, she waited for someone to pick up on the other end.

Her wait wasn't long.

"Hello? Uncle Andrew?" The word *uncle* still felt foreign on her tongue, but she was getting more accustomed to it and she had to admit she liked the whole concept, liked the way it made her feel to be part of something bigger than just herself and her brothers. "This is Greer. I was wondering if you'd mind having three extra at the table for dinner tonight?"

"Mind? You obviously haven't been part of the family long enough," the man on the other end of the line told her with a pleased laugh. "C'mon over," he urged heartily. "The more the better."

"What time's dinner?" she wanted to know.

The answer was one that she would eventually learn to expect. "What time can you get here?"

Greer didn't bother trying to hold back the smile that rose to her lips. The man was every bit the legend he was made out to be. Warm and generous to a fault. The father figure every family patriarch *should* be.

"Just so you know," she told the former chief of police, "I'll be bringing Judge Blake Kincannon and his father."

"Thanks for telling me," he answered. "I'll make a point of calling Callie and telling her that Brent's presence is requested."

She was vaguely aware that Callie, Andrew's oldest daughter, was married to a judge. The two had met several years ago when Callie was assigned to find his kidnapped daughter.

"That's really not necessary," Greer assured the patriarch.

Andrew saw it differently. "Of course it is. Your judge gets to talk to another judge and Rose and I get a reason to make our daughter and her family drop by. It's a win-win situation."

They were right, Greer thought. There was no arguing with Andrew Cavanaugh. Not that she really wanted to. "We'll be there in forty minutes," Greer promised.

"Any time is fine," he answered as he broke the connection.

"We'll be where in forty minutes?" Blake wanted to know.

She would have had to have been deaf to miss the edge in his voice. "At Andrew Cavanaugh's house. We're invited to dinner."

"You invited yourself over," Blake pointed out. He was far from pleased with the turn of events. When not in court, he tended to prefer staying at home to going anywhere.

"Just beating Uncle Andrew to the punch," she told him cheerfully. "If I'd stayed on the phone long enough, he would have been the one doing the inviting. He really likes nothing better than to have a full house at every meal."

It was one of the first things she'd learned about the former chief of police. The only thing Andrew Cavanaugh loved more than cooking was having his family and friends over, eating his cooking. Any time, night or day, there was always something on the stove, always an extra chair to be pulled up at the custom-built, extra-long table.

No one who came over ever left hungry—or lonely.

"That's all well and good," Kincannon told her, a note of finality in his voice, "but I'm staying in tonight."

"You can stay in after we get back," she informed him cheerfully.

His eyes narrowed, darkening. "Detective, as I understand your assignment, you're supposed to guard me, not order me around."

"I have to do whatever it takes to keep you safe and well," she countered. "In case you're wondering, this comes under the 'well' heading."

He had no intentions of giving in. If he gave this woman an inch, he was certain that he was going to lose the proverbial mile.

"Look, Detective, my life's disrupted enough already. Much as I might appreciate the gesture, I don't feel like dropping everything and running over to the former chief's house."

To Greer's surprise, it was Alexander who came to her aid. "Oh, lighten up, Blake. You're not running anywhere, she's driving us. Right, O'Brien?"

"That's the deal," she answered with a broad smile. And then she turned to the judge. "I'll make you a bargain, Your Honor. You come with me tonight and tomorrow, I'll get someone on the squad to go shopping for me and I'll make dinner here."

"You cook?" Blake asked in surprise. A woman who looked as good as she did didn't have to know how to cook. He could see men falling all over themselves for the privilege of wining and dining her.

"Almost as good as Uncle Andrew," she said with just the right touch of modesty.

He did his best to remain steadfast, although he felt the ground beneath his feet turning to sand. And the vibrant detective who probably had no clue that she was getting to him at the speed of light was the sandstorm. Damn, under any other circumstances…but it was what it was and he had to remember that. This was a professional situation. He couldn't allow himself to let it get personal. Or intimate.

"That's not necessary."

"You let me be the judge of that—no disrespect intended," Greer added.

"None taken." This time, the judge fairly growled his response.

"Good, you came. We can get started," Andrew Cavanaugh declared heartily less than thirty minutes

later. Rubbing his hands together in anticipatory pleasure, Andrew had walked out to greet Greer and his
other two guests just as she pulled her vehicle up into
the driveway.

Andrew positioned himself on the passenger side of
the sedan so that Blake and his father had no choice but
to greet him and shake the hand that the former police
chief offered.

"Hello," he said warmly, "I'm Andrew Cavanaugh,
Greer's uncle, and this is my wife, Rose." He nodded at
the youthful-looking woman beside him.

The man was a hell of a lot more than that, Greer
couldn't help thinking. He ran a 24/7 kitchen and was a
saint to boot. Everyone in the family turned to him when
they needed emotional support. That was definitely far
and away more important than just being her uncle.

But hearing Andrew say it sent a warm, happy
feeling through her, as if, for the first time in her life,
she actually belonged somewhere.

"Alexander Kincannon," the older man said, taking
Andrew's offered hand first. "Gunny to my friends."

"I hope I'll number among those."

"Let me try your cooking and we'll see," Alexander
responded half seriously.

"I'm Blake Kincannon." Leaning forward, Blake
shook his host's hand. "You'll have to excuse my father,"
he apologized, slanting an irritated glance at Alexander.
"He doesn't get out much."

"Look who's talking," Alexander hooted. "If it wasn't
for going to court, I'd have to start referring to you as
The Shadow."

The reference was to an illusive comic book hero from the forties, but from the knowing look on Andrew's face it was clear he was familiar with it. Very neatly, the man got in between father and son, a human barrier to their escalating exchange of words.

"Judge," he said to Blake, "I took the liberty of inviting my son-in-law over. Brent's a sitting judge and I thought the two of you might have things in common to talk about."

He knew of only one Brent on the bench. "Brenton Montgomery?" Blake asked.

"Right here," a deep voice announced from the family room. The next moment, Brent had crossed over to his father-in-law's newest converts.

Greer caught Andrew's eye and mouthed, "Thank you," gratitude flowing from every pore. She knew the situation was tense for the two men she'd brought, but the last thing she wanted was a verbal confrontation between them.

She should have known she could count on Andrew not just to defuse the situation, but to generate a feeling of well-being, not only verbally, but also with the food he so deftly prepared.

Uttering a deep, satisfied sigh, Alexander Kincannon pushed himself away from the table after having consumed three generous helpings of the lamb stew that Andrew had prepared.

"You know, every time I've had a man cook for me, it's been less than a memorable experience," he confided, raising his eyes to look at his host. "Can't say that anymore. Well, I can," the man amended with a small grin. "But then I'd be lying. This has to be the best meal I've had, bar none, in more years than I can clearly remember. You do have a gift, Andy," he announced as if it were a new discovery, "you surely do."

"Thank you, Gunny. I take that as very high praise. Feel free to drop by anytime." Andrew turned toward the man Greer was guarding. "Same goes for you, Blake."

"Thank you, Chief." Blake glanced toward Greer. "But it looks like I'll have to get permission from my keeper, first."

Callie smiled as she looked quizzically at her newfound cousin. "Greer? Is there something you'd like to share with the group?" she deadpanned.

For some reason, the subject of the exact manner of the relationship between her and the judge and his father hadn't come up during dinner. To her relief, it turned out that Brent and Blake knew each other. The two men had gotten caught up in a conversation that revolved around a recent controversial court ruling. The others at the table added their own opinions and, for a while, it was just a typical Cavanaugh dinner where not only the food but the company was enjoyed.

As discretely as possible, Greer took a breath before answering. "I'm the judge's bodyguard," she told Callie, trying her best to sound matter-of-fact about the assignment.

A glance toward Andrew told her that the Cavanaugh patriarch already knew about the arranged relationship, as did his wife. But this was obviously news to his daughter and her husband.

For a second, Brent looked thunderstruck, and then he laughed at his own ignorance. "Of course. That was your courtroom on the news, wasn't it?"

Blake sighed. He was beginning to wonder, even at this early date, if he was ever going to hear the end of this.

"Yes, that was mine."

Callie was immediately sympathetic. "You were lucky you weren't hurt."

Blake looked at Greer, remembering. "Luck didn't have anything to do with it. I was tackled by Detective O'Brien in order to get me out of the line of fire," he told the others.

"I'd still call that luck," Andrew told him. "She could have been half a second slower to react and you could be lying in a drawer in the morgue right now, waiting to be cut open."

Alexander looked from his son to the woman he had taken almost an instant shine to.

"*She* tackled *you?*" he asked, clearly in awe of the information. He shook his head as if the information didn't compute. "But she's just a bit of a thing."

"I wouldn't underestimate her if I were you, Gunny," Andrew warned with a laugh. He slipped an arm around Rose to underscore his words. "The Cavanaugh women might look petite, but underneath all that softness, they're as hard as steel."

"Not completely," Brent corrected, exchanging a look with his wife that silently spoke volumes.

He could vouch for that, Blake caught himself thinking. The next moment, he banished the unexpected thought—and the memory it summoned—from his mind. It was time to get going—and to terminate this social gathering. Being around O'Brien this way was creating havoc with his thoughts.

Blake cleared his throat. "Chief Cavanaugh, as my father said, that was a really wonderful meal. But I'm afraid that I have to—"

Andrew was way ahead of him. He nodded understandingly. "You need to get back home. Of course. I won't keep you," he assured his guest, rising to his feet. Rising beside him, Rose began clearing away the dishes. Callie and Brent both joined her.

Feeling guilty, Greer began to follow suit only to have Andrew take the plates out of her hands and shift them over toward his son-in-law. "Tonight you're not just family, Greer," he told her. "Tonight you're a guest, as well."

The way she saw it, she'd imposed on his hospitality, bringing two more mouths for him to feed. The least she could do was help clean up.

"But I—" Greer got no further in her protest.

"No argument," he instructed with finality. "Next time I'll let you pick up twice as many plates," he promised with a wink. "But right now, you have to take the judge and his father home."

"Don't even try to argue," Rose told her. "The man still wears his badge pinned to his bare chest at night. He's used to being obeyed."

Andrew merely smiled. "Some habits are harder to break than others," he told his guests. "I'll walk you to the door," he volunteered, ushering Greer, the judge and his father to the foyer. He stopped just outside the threshold. "Now that you know the way, Judge, don't be a stranger. You, too, Gunny."

Blake looked at his host and realized that the man actually meant what he was saying. He *wanted* them to come by. Why? Despite the evening that they'd just shared, he and his father were all but strangers to Andrew Cavanaugh. Why would the former chief of police welcome them so warmly into his home?

He had no answer. Neither did he know where this quiet feeling of well-being that was softly whispering through him had come from. He decided, for the time being, to stop analyzing it and just enjoy the sensation for as long as it lasted.

Blake refrained from shaking his head, but he was still rather mystified.

Strange people, strange evening.

And, as he and his father walked to O'Brien's sedan, Blake had more than a fleeting suspicion that this wasn't going to be the last strange evening he was going to spend.

# Chapter 7

Former gunnery sergeant Alexander Kincannon frowned as he watched the young woman in his living room remove the leather and suede decorative pillows that had been on the sofa.

"Don't seem right," he commented to Greer, "you spending the night on the couch. That's supposed to be strictly for husbands who've had cross words with their wives. Y'know, punishment. Not that I've had any experience with that."

"Didn't think you did." Greer hid her smile as she turned away, stacking the second pillow on top of the first. "Don't worry, Mr. Kincannon. I'll be fine."

His frown deepened just for a moment. "You got a learning disability, girl?" he asked. "I told you to call me Gunny."

She wasn't accustomed to being so familiar with a

man the senior Kincannon's age. It was hard enough for her to adjust to Andrew and his brother. "Sorry. 'Gunny,'" Greer acquiesced. "The sofa is more than adequate for my needs."

"It's not comfortable," he insisted. To prove his point, Alexander hit the cushion with the flat of his hand. It didn't give the way something that was a sofa would. "Fell asleep on that once, watching TV. It was like sleeping on a board."

Greer had a feeling that the man had fallen asleep watching TV more than once, but she kept that to herself. "That suits my purposes just fine. I don't want to be comfortable, I want to be on my guard," she reminded the judge's father.

Just then, the judge entered the room. His arms were filled with bedding. "So if this assignment runs a week—God forbid—you're planning to be awake the whole time? What are you, a zombie or one of the *undead* that seem to be so popular these days?"

Turning around to face him, Greer grinned. "Sorry to disappoint you, but I'm neither."

She was certainly acting as if she thought she was one of those creatures, he thought. "But you don't plan on sleeping."

"Catnaps," she interjected before he could continue. "I get by on catnaps."

Now there was a misnomer for an event if he ever heard one. "Every cat I ever knew spent most of the day 'napping.'"

The man was testy and argumentative. Was it just because she was here, or was there something more going on? They'd been here for only the past couple of hours and as far as she knew, nothing had changed. After dinner, she'd entertained the hope that he was coming around and that would make things easier on all of them.

Obviously not.

"Short catnaps," she emphasized.

Blake put down the bedding he'd gotten from the hall closet upstairs. There was a pillow, a blanket and two sheets. He nodded at the sagging stack. "Will you need anything else?"

"I don't think I'll even need this." Pulling the blanket out of the pile, she held it out to him. "It doesn't get cold this time of year," she explained tactfully.

He knew that. Did she think he lived in a bubble? "That was to put on top of the seat cushions and under the sheet to make it more comfortable for you—but I forgot, you don't want to be comfortable."

Ignoring the slight sarcastic tone, Greer continued to hold the blanket out to him. "I appreciate the thought, Judge."

Alexander seemed to realize the inequity of the situation. "Shouldn't there be two of you?" he wanted to know.

"Don't think the world is ready for that," Blake muttered under his breath.

Overhearing, Greer grinned before she could think better of it. "Once the dust settles, the arrangement will be reviewed," she assured the older man. "Most likely, my partner will be sharing the assignment."

Tufted eyebrows rose in hopeful query. "Another woman?"

Greer shook her head. "Sorry to disappoint you, Gunny. Not even on his best day." Taking the fitted sheet, she tucked it around the three seat cushions, swiftly preparing a makeshift bed for when she needed to use it. "You can go about your regular routine," she told the two men when neither of them moved but continued watching her. "Pretend I'm not even here. Think of me the way you think of your security system."

Blake took the opportunity to leave the room. He had work waiting for him in his den.

"Never thought of the security system as having killer legs," Alexander said, half to himself, half to her.

Greer laughed. "That's one of the nicest things anyone ever said to me," she told the older Kincannon. The man cleared his throat and grumbled under his breath in an attempt to disguise the fact that her response pleased him.

"You up to watching some TV?" Alexander wanted to know as he reached for the remote control.

"Sounds like a plan to me," she told him agreeably. Gunny sat down in the corner of the sofa he favored. After a beat, Greer joined him.

Fifteen seconds later, after the initial warm-up period, a commercial for a popular orange juice was literally splashed across the forty-six-inch flat screen. It was gone in an instant as Alexander, employing the remote, began channel surfing.

Suddenly, he seemed to realize that he wasn't alone. Grudgingly, Gunny held out the remote to her.

Rather than take it, Greer shook her head. "You're doing just fine without me."

"You don't mind my flying through the channels?" he asked, surprised.

"Your house, your prerogative," Greer told him, paraphrasing what his son had said to her when he refused to stay in the courtroom but joined her in trying to run down the escaping prisoner.

Fresh admiration entered the bright blue eyes as they crinkled. "You're all right, O'Brien." Alexander chuckled.

"Thank you." She inclined her head in acknowledgment of his words. "I take that as a very high compliment, Gunny."

He made a small, dismissive noise, uncomfortable with anything remotely resembling gratitude. "That's the way it was intended. Now watch the screen," he instructed gruffly, pointing toward the monitor with his remote.

Unable to concentrate because of the woman who was spending the night in his house, Blake gave up trying to work a little more than an hour into what had turned out to be a futile endeavor.

Biting off an oath, he closed the law book he'd been searching through—using books had always been far more satisfying to him than searching for information on the Internet. Try as he might, he still couldn't bring himself to trust something he couldn't hold in his hand.

Picking the fat tome up, he was about to place it back

on the shelf behind his desk when he stopped. He'd leave it on his desk until tomorrow, he decided. With any luck, he'd be able to get his thoughts together then.

With a little more luck than that, he'd be minus one houseguest.

Not that, under a completely different set of circumstances, he wouldn't have found her startlingly attractive. He would and, if he were being strictly honest with himself, he did. There were times when he felt that her incredibly light blue eyes saw right through him. She had the face of an angel, albeit a sexy angel, and a body made for sin.

Detective Greer O'Brien was definitely not a run-of-the-mill, ordinary woman who he could easily come across any day of the week.

He didn't know of any women who were willing to take a bullet for him.

But as noble as that might be, it also pointed to the fact that she was impulsive and impetuous. Which made her an unknown element in his life. He really didn't need that. And the sooner she was gone, the sooner he could get on with his life—such as it was.

Blake sighed. He found her presence in his house disturbing on so many levels. Until O'Brien had come crashing into him, landing on top as she brought him down, he'd thought that he'd completely shut down after Margaret's death. Shut down as a man. If he had needs, they were on such a deep, faraway level that he was not aware of them.

Or hadn't been until this morning.

Something else to hold against Detective O'Brien, he thought with another sigh.

Getting up, Blake crossed to the den's threshold and shut off the light. He could literally feel the tension. It was riding roughshod throughout his whole body, making his neck and shoulders ache as well as unsettling various other parts of him, physically and emotionally.

He really didn't need this.

What he did need was a good night's sleep. Maybe that would help him put some of this to rest. But as he started to go toward the stairs, he paused. He could hear the TV in the living room. It sounded like a Western.

Was his father still up?

Curiosity had Blake making his way into the living room. As he'd suspected, his father was still up. Or rather, propped up. The crusty old man had nodded off, as was his habit sometimes.

And he'd been right about the TV program. There was some old, classic Western playing on the set. His father favored Westerns, complaining that the current crop of filmmakers didn't have a clue how to make a decent one. For last Christmas, he'd gifted the old man with a complete DVD collection of John Wayne's more famous Westerns. Alexander Kincannon knew the dialogue to every one of them.

"You don't have to keep watching that," Blake told his unwanted houseguest as he walked up behind her. "My father's asleep."

She smiled, looking at her dozing companion. There was a note of affection in her voice as she told Blake,

"He lasted about fifteen minutes. It's probably the food. Eating as much as he did tonight makes a person sleepy."

"So does being in his early seventies," the judge pointed out. Right now, he mused, it was hard to believe that he was looking at a decorated war hero. His father seemed so docile. "I'll take him up to bed," he told her, stooping for a moment so that he could take one of his father's arms and slip it over his shoulders for leverage. He rose slowly, bringing the man up with him. The channel on the set remained the same. Still asleep, his father grunted as Blake brought him to his feet. "I said you didn't have to watch that," he told Greer again.

"I heard you, Judge." She made no effort to reach for the remote. "I happen to like Westerns."

One arm tucked around his father's midriff, the other holding the man's arm over his shoulders, Blake paused for a moment, studying her.

And then he shook his head. "You're a strange woman, Detective O'Brien."

Greer flashed a grin. "I've been told that. And if we're going to be housemates for a few days, you might as well call me Greer. It's less cumbersome on the tongue."

The word *tongue* set his imagination off before he could rein it in. Like slowly running his along the slope of her neck—and parts beyond. A warmth came over him. He wasn't having very pillar-of-the-community-like thoughts.

Had to be because he was tired, he thought defensively.

"Greer," he repeated. Not an ordinary name. Not an

ordinary woman, he thought as he began to slowly guide his father away from the sofa.

"Need help?" she offered.

"I've done this before," he answered. Then, after a beat, he added, "But thanks for offering."

The corners of her mouth curved. That cost him, she thought. The man was human, but it cost him. "Don't mention it."

Roused, his father opened one sleepy eye. "Movie over?" he wanted to know, mumbling his words. Releasing a huge sigh, he all but sank to his knees. Blake tightened his arm around the older man's waist.

"Yup," Blake lied.

Alexander's eyes drooped down again, shutting. "Who won?"

"The good guys, Dad," Blake answered. "Work with me here, Dad. We're coming to the first step."

"Step," Alexander repeated without any comprehension of the word. But he did raise his foot obligingly.

His back was to her and Blake couldn't see it, but he would have sworn that he *felt* the detective's smile widening.

After spending a generally restless, fitful night, Blake decided to get an early start on the day. As he came down the next morning, the aroma of fresh coffee greeted him. Fresh coffee and a scent he couldn't immediately place. All he knew was that it wasn't anything he'd smelled in the morning in his own house.

Not since before Margaret died.

Had to be his imagination, he told himself. That momentary sexual awakening he'd experienced yesterday had played havoc with his senses. That obviously included his sense of smell, he concluded.

His eyes shifted toward the sofa as he passed by the living room.

It was empty.

The bedding he'd given the detective was now neatly folded and stacked on a corner of the sofa.

Was she gone?

He doubted if he was going to be that lucky.

Making his way into the kitchen, he saw that he was right. She was in the kitchen, talking to his father. The aroma of freshly brewed coffee was her doing, he suspected.

How? As far as he knew, there was no coffee in the house.

As he walked in, his father turned and looked over his shoulder at him. "Pull up a chair, Blake. O'Brien's making us breakfast."

Confused, Blake looked down at the scrambled eggs with bits of ham that the detective had just put on a second plate—his, he assumed.

"Breakfast?" he echoed. "Out of what?" he wanted to know. "I'm fairly certain there's no recipe that turns beer into scrambled eggs and coffee." Nonetheless, he eased himself into the chair that was opposite the one his father was in. "Miracles a sideline of yours, Greer? Or did you sneak out to the grocery store early this morning?"

Leaving him and his father unattended would be

committing a dereliction of duty and they both knew it. *Trying to trip me up, Judge?* she wondered.

"Neither," she replied cheerfully. "Uncle Andrew had Aunt Rose slip some basic supplies into the trunk of my car when we weren't paying attention. He told me what he did just as we were leaving. I put them into the refrigerator when you were working in the den."

So that was what the chief had whispered to O'Brien last night. No doubt about it—the family was strange. "I earn a decent salary," he told her. "I don't need charity, however well intentioned."

She felt herself growing protective of the family patriarch—not that he needed her to defend him. She supposed that meant that she was really becoming a Cavanaugh.

"Uncle Andrew doesn't see it as charity. He calls it sharing. My new half sister, Patience, tells me that it's a habit of his. To refuse is an insult," she added.

Too busy eating and enjoying his breakfast, Alexander had remained silent during the exchange. Swallowing now, he put in his two cents.

"Try this, Blake," he urged, pushing the other plate closer to his son. "It's damn good." And then Alexander turned his attention to the woman who had so unexpectedly come into their lives, and, as far as he was concerned, brightened them. "You weren't kidding when you said you could cook."

"No point in lying about something like that," she answered, pleased that he seemed to be enjoying her efforts so much. She noticed that the judge left his plate untouched.

She got him a cup of coffee. Leaving it black, she moved it next to his plate and waited.

"You married, O'Brien?" Alexander asked her without warning.

"No." She'd come close once or twice, but then she'd come to her senses and broken it off. Relationships made her uneasy. They required too much commitment and yielded too much disappointment.

"Spoken for?" the senior Kincannon prodded.

"Dad," Blake said sharply. Alexander didn't appear to hear.

"No," Greer answered the older man's question.

Alexander pinned her with a look and asked, half seriously, "How do you feel about a retired marine?"

Unable to keep it back any longer, Greer allowed a smile to emerge. Humor danced in her eyes. "Respectful."

Greer answered the older man's question just as his son uttered another, far more exasperated, "Dad!"

What the hell had gotten into his father? Blake wondered. Yes, the woman was attractive, and yes, there was something about her that transcended the sum of her parts, something that could readily arouse a man if he wasn't careful, but he gave his father more credit than to behave like a smitten adolescent.

"Fella's got a right to know if he's got a chance," Alexander answered, clearly annoyed that his son felt he had to reprimand him like some errant kid. The retired marine shifted his attention back to Greer. "Do I?" The twinkle in his eye told her he was teasing her.

Greer shook her head. "I'm afraid you're just too young for me, Gunny."

Before either father or son could make a comment, Greer's cell phone began to ring. Putting down the spatula she was holding, she took the phone out of her pocket and flipped it open.

Turning her back to the two men she'd just served, Greer said, "This is Detective O'Brien."

Her partner didn't waste time with greetings or preambles. This wasn't a social call. "They found the stolen ambulance." His tone indicated that it wasn't a good find.

The bailiff's frightened face flashed through her mind. Greer tensed. "And?"

She heard Jeff take a breath before answering. "The bailiff was still inside."

She made the only logical guess she could. "Dead?"

"No, not then. The kid hung on long enough to reach the hospital. But he died on the operating table," Jeff told her.

What a waste. The second he'd agreed to help Munro escape, he'd been a dead man. It was all just a matter of when the bullet would find him. "Did he say anything before he died?"

"Yeah, as a matter of fact, he did. He said to tell the judge he was sorry, but he had to do it. They threatened to kill his family."

There was no comfort in knowing she'd guessed right. The man was still dead before he'd had a chance to live.

"And?" she prodded when Jeff didn't continue. "What about the family? Were they at the house?"

"Yeah." There was a long pause. "The wife was shot dead," Jeff told her grimly.

She felt her stomach tightening into a hard knot. "And the baby?" Greer forced herself to ask. Her voice came out in a whisper.

"Seems Munro—or one of his people at any rate—draws the line at killing babies," her partner answered. "The police found the baby wet and dirty and screaming…but alive. The chief's got your brother looking for the bailiff's next of kin."

A family man even in the worst of times, she thought. "Which one?" she asked.

There was momentary silence on the other end. And then Jeff answered, "Whichever one he can find."

"No, I mean which brother has he got out looking for the next of kin?"

She heard Jeff laugh shortly. "Oh, yeah, I forgot, you've got two of them. Ethan. And there's more news," he continued. "Someone tampered with the judge's car. It blew up when it was started. The officer never stood a chance." Greer closed her eyes. She'd had a feeling. Damn but there were days she hated being right. "By the way," Jeff was saying, "how's the babysitting detail going?"

"Better than it went for the bailiff and the officer," she commented darkly. And then, because she had to ask even though she had a feeling she already knew the answer, Greer asked, "No sign of Munro?"

"If there was, I would have told you that right off the bat," Jeff said.

"I was hoping you were saving the best was for last," Greer told him with a sigh. "Keep me posted."

"Will do." And with that, her partner broke the connection.

When she turned around again, slipping her phone back into her pocket, she found Blake staring at her.

"Tell me." The words came from Blake. It wasn't a request. It was an order.

## Chapter 8

Blake's somber expression masked his thoughts as he listened to the sketchy details of what had happened to his bailiff, Tim Kelly, and the fact that his car had been wired to blow up the moment he started it. He made no comment during her swift narrative.

Kincannon looked almost preoccupied, but Greer knew better. The judge had heard and digested every word she'd said.

"And Tim's little girl?" he asked quietly. "Where is she?"

This, at least, she thought, was somewhat positive. "The chief of detectives is trying to locate the bailiff's next of kin before the social services system has a chance to swallow her up."

Blake nodded, taking the information in. They all knew that once a child was within the system, there were miles of red tape to untangle before that child could be extricated.

"Tim has—had," the judge corrected himself and she could see that the bailiff's death and the manner in which it happened had affected him far more deeply than the destruction of his vehicle, "an aunt who raised him. She lives in Santa Barbara." He paused, thinking. "Donna McClosky, I think he said her name was."

Greer had her phone out again. "This is really going to help, Judge," she told him. Two seconds later, her partner answered and she passed the information on. After terminating the call, she flipped the phone shut and tucked it away. "My partner's going to let the chief know what you said and get right on it." She paused for a second, debating asking the next question. Curiosity got the better of her. "You were close to the bailiff?" she asked, studying his expression.

Blake heard the note of sympathy in her voice. He didn't respond well to sympathy. It was too close to pity and that reminded him of other things.

Looking away, he shrugged carelessly. "He talked, I listened. Close?" he repeated the word, as if weighing it. "No. But he was young and enthusiastic and extremely likeable." He deliberately drew the focus away from himself by adding, "Everyone who knew him could tell you that."

Quietly sipping his black coffee, listening, his father looked at him. "Sounds like Scottie," Alexander commented.

"Scottie?" This was a new name, one she was unfamiliar with. Greer looked from one man to the other, waiting for one of them to enlighten her. By the look on his face, she had a feeling that her answer wasn't going to come from the judge.

"My younger son," Alexander told her stoically.

The older man, she noted, was staring at the remaining black liquid in his cup, avoiding her eyes. This was the first she'd heard of a sibling. "You have a brother?" she asked Blake.

"Had," Blake corrected tersely, grinding out the word almost against his will.

She waited for details, and, as she expected, it was the older Kincannon who ultimately filled her in. "Scottie was killed saving his platoon in Afghanistan. He was a marine," his father said with pride.

"He died a hero," Greer concluded.

Blake's face was stony. "Bottom line, he died," he said, his voice hollow.

A wave of compassion washed over her. Kincannon certainly had had his share of tragedies, she thought, her heart going out to him.

"A hero," Alexander repeated firmly, daring his remaining son to contradict him.

Blake had no desire to get into an argument this early in the morning. Scottie had wanted nothing more than their father's approval and had rushed off to enlist to fight for his country the minute he graduated college. It had been an utter waste of a decent human being.

Stifling a sigh, Blake echoed, "A hero," and let it go at that. He looked at Greer. "When you get Donna McClosky's address, let me know."

"So you can send her your condolences?" Greer

asked, thinking that Kincannon was a nicer man than he wanted people to believe.

Blake didn't answer at first, debating how much information to part with. But, given what he was learning about this woman's nature, he knew that she'd make it a point to find out. He might as well spare himself the interrogation.

"Costs a lot to raise a child these days. From what Tim told me, his aunt was just barely getting by. He was looking for a second job so he could send her a little money every month."

"You're gonna set up some kind of a trust fund for the kid?" It was a rhetorical question on his father's part. "Count me in."

Blake looked at his father. The only income the older man had was his pension. "You don't exactly have money to burn, Gunny."

His father's grin was a bit lopsided. "Yeah, I know, but I got this kid who lets me live at his place free. Been saving up for something special. This trust fund just might be it," he added with a nod of his head.

Generosity with a minimum of words. And a maximum of heart. For a moment, a surge of emotion threatened to close her throat. Yesterday, in court, when she sat in the witness chair, Kincannon had struck her as a somber, humorless man, a man who had evolved without a heart because of the loss he'd suffered. She would have never guessed that there was this caring side to him.

Just goes to show, you never really know about a person. "I'll get you that address," she promised.

"Good." Blake began to rise.

Greer was instantly alert. "Where are you going, Judge?"

"I have this flowing black robe." There was more than a touch of sarcasm in his voice. "It only seems to go with a courtroom as an accessory."

She ignored the sarcasm. "It's early, Judge," she pointed out, then indicated his plate. He'd barely touched it. "And you haven't eaten your breakfast yet."

"Won't go to waste," Alexander was quick to tell her, eyeing the plate. "I'll eat it if he's fool enough not to."

"No, he'll eat it," she told the other man, looking pointedly at Blake. "You wouldn't want to hurt my feelings, would you, Judge?"

Blake laughed shortly. "I don't think that's possible."

"You'd be surprised." That had slipped out unintentionally. She hurried to cover it up. There was no way she was going to let the judge think that she had a sensitive side. "At least try it," she urged. "I'll make you a deal. If you don't like it, you don't have to finish it."

With a sigh, Blake sat down again, resigned. "If I don't go along with this, you're probably going to try to force-feed me, saying something inane about a plane and an air hanger."

"Actually, I was considering a train and a tunnel, but a plane and an air hanger work just as well." Her straight face lasted only halfway through the sentence. The grin that took over threatened to split her face in half. "It won't hurt you to have something in your stomach,

Judge," she added seriously. "Think of it as a way to help you put up with the morning."

His eyes met hers as he raised the fork to his lips. "It's not the morning I have to put up with." There was no mistaking his meaning.

Rather than comment, Greer looked at Blake's father. He appeared amused by the exchange. "Is your son always this surly in the morning?" she wanted to know.

The shaggy gray head nodded sadly. "Afraid so, O'Brien. He's like this most mornings. Sometimes worse."

She took a breath and let it out, as if that somehow helped her fortify herself. "Something to look forward to."

"You realize that you don't have to," Blake pointed out. "No one's holding *you* prisoner."

She caught his meaning. "You're not a prisoner, Judge," she told him with all sincerity. "It just so happens that you and your father are two very special people that the Aurora police department would like to see continue living." She nodded at his plate. "So, how was it?"

He didn't follow her. "How was what?"

"Breakfast." When he didn't reply immediately, she realized that he'd consumed it all without even being aware of what he was doing. The man was definitely a challenge. "You finished it."

Blake looked down at his plate, a mild look of surprise momentarily slipping across his features. He didn't even remember chewing or swallowing, but he obviously must have. His plate was empty.

The woman was apparently still waiting for an evaluation of her culinary skills. "All right I guess. I'm still standing."

"High praise indeed," Greer said dryly. "But just for the record, Judge, you're sitting."

Pushing back his chair, Blake rose to his feet. "And now I'm standing."

Greer laughed, shaking her head. If she looked up *contrary* in the dictionary, she had a sneaking suspicion that she'd find Kincannon's handsome face staring back at her.

"Just no end to your talents, is there, Judge?"

He made no reply; instead, he asked a question. With nothing to lose, he thought he'd take a shot. "Any chance of my going to the courthouse alone?"

She flashed him a serene smile. "About as much chance as my growing two feet and playing on the Lakers by next season."

"What about my father?" He nodded at the elder Kincannon, fairly certain that he finally had her. "He doesn't go to court with me. How are you going to guard him *and* me? Even you can't be two places at the same time."

If he thought he was baiting her, he was going to be disappointed. "I am aware of that, Judge. I passed high-school physics with flying colors," she replied. "I have someone coming to stay with your father while we're at the courthouse."

She heard her former ally groan behind her. As she turned around, he said, "No offense, O'Brien, but I don't take kindly to being handed off."

Glancing at her watch, she noted the time. Taylor should be getting here at any moment. "I know, which is why I requested Taylor McIntyre for the job." She'd called the chief last night, right after the Kincannons had gone to bed. She had a feeling that Taylor would have more luck handling Gunny. The ex-marine might grumble about having women in charge, but he definitely responded to the female touch.

The doorbell suddenly rang. The cavalry had arrived. "And there she is."

"She?" Alexander echoed, instantly perking up.

She'd made the right decision, Greer thought. She glanced at the man over her shoulder, doing her best to suppress an amused grin. "Oh, didn't I mention that Taylor was a woman?" she asked innocently. "She's also the chief of detectives' stepdaughter."

"Anyone on the police force *not* related to Chief Cavanaugh?" Blake wanted to know. It seemed like the entire force was peppered with his relatives.

"There's got to be a couple of people," she deadpanned as she went to the door.

Greer opened it cautiously, acutely aware that even though she was expecting her step-cousin at this time, it still might be one of Munro's lackeys standing on the doorstep.

Fortunately, it was just Taylor.

The other woman did her best to summon a smile, or at least one that generally resembled one in passing. It took obvious effort.

"I'm not a morning person," Taylor warned by way of a greeting as she walked in.

Greer glanced at the judge. Taylor wasn't the only one, she thought. "There's a lot of that going around," she commented under her breath, then said with more feeling, "You should feel right at home."

Turning to the two men she'd spent the night with, Greer made introductions. "Taylor, this is Judge Blake Kincannon and his father, former gunnery sergeant Alexander Kincannon, retired marine," she added, knowing that the reference would put the older man in a good, hopefully cooperative mood. "Gentlemen, this is Detective Taylor McIntyre—" she looked deliberately at Alexander "—soon to be Detective Taylor Laredo."

"That's Cavanaugh-Laredo," Taylor corrected with a yawn. "I've decided to get my name legally changed." She saw the other woman looking at her in mild surprise. "Seems only right since Brian was more of a father to me, my brothers and sister than the guy who lent us his gene pool," she explained. Not waiting on ceremony, she purloined Greer's mug. There was still approximately four ounces of coffee in it.

Taylor drained it in less than five seconds. Putting the cup down, she asked Greer belatedly, "You didn't want that, did you?"

"Not half as much as you did," she assured the senior detective.

"You're getting married?" Alexander asked the new woman, interested.

Taylor beamed, her thoughts clearly straying to the man she was engaged to. Her devotion to her future husband was no secret. In fact, she'd once even confided that her fiancé could instantly raise her body temperature by five degrees with just a promising look. "As soon as we can set a date," she told the judge's father.

As if foiled, Alexander turned his attention back to Greer. "Looks like I'm just going to have to wear you down, O'Brien." He chuckled.

He wasn't going to stand here while his father all but made a fool of himself. "Time to go," Blake announced. "Nice meeting you, Detective." He nodded at the woman he was leaving with his father. She had his full sympathy, he thought.

"The pleasure was all mine," Taylor assured him. She stepped back beside her assignment for the day. "See you tonight," she told Greer. The glint in her blue eyes told Greer that she considered her new step-cousin's assignment the better one by at least a country mile.

Greer pretended she didn't notice.

With the Munro trial bumped indefinitely, Judge Kincannon's administrative assistant was forced to reschedule all the other cases and move them up on the calendar. Consequently, this morning, the judge found himself facing a child molester whose lawyer actually provided the defense that when his client indulged in recreational drugs, they turned the man into a completely different person. And it was *that* person who was the child molester. A stint in rehab, the lawyer declared, should clear everything all up.

It was all Blake could do to keep his ever increasing disdain for the defendant and his alleged crime from showing on his face. But at his core, Kincannon was a firm believer that everyone deserved their day in court and that they also deserved to be represented by competent counsel.

He was well aware of cases where the wrong man or woman was sent away for a crime they didn't commit. To his knowledge, his cases didn't number among them. He'd like to think that it was because he tried to keep proceedings as fair as possible, but he knew that there was also a good amount of luck involved.

He hoped to God that his luck never ran out.

It had been an extremely long day, broken up only by a quick recess for lunch, part of which was spent mediating a point of conflict for yet another set of counselors. When Blake finally got around to eating, he sent out for sandwiches from a local sandwich shop and had them brought to his chambers.

Ordinarily, he ate alone, usually at his desk. Most of the time, he would also be reviewing something that required his attention.

Today, though, he'd had to share his precious so-called free time with his bodyguard. It didn't sit that well with him. He valued the moments he was alone with his thoughts. With Greer, there was no such thing as being alone.

There was also no such thing as silence.

The woman seemed to actively have something against the latter because any time silence threatened to break out, she began talking again, filling the air with words to the point that Blake felt as if he was literally under attack. Occasionally, she came up for air, but that hardly seemed to last more than a couple of minutes at a time, and then she launched yet another verbal discourse.

Court was over for the day and they were now on their way home—and still she continued prattling on.

There was a headache behind his eyes that threatened to take over at any moment. He turned toward the woman in the driver's seat and asked, "Have you ever tried yoga, Detective?"

She wasn't into sitting quietly in a twisted position. Weight-lifting and cross-training were far more her style. "Once," she admitted, unaware that a slight frown slipped over her lips. "I didn't like it."

Blake sighed. It figured. "I had a feeling," he said, more to himself than to her.

"I'm not the type to sit around and mediate." She suspected he'd already guessed that, but she said it anyway. "I'm more of a doer." She extended it to her job. That was, after all, what she was doing here. Her job. "I like being out in the field, rounding up dealers—"

He had a feeling that this current assignment was going to drive her crazy if it extended beyond a couple of days. That made two of them.

"Then what are you doing here?" Blake asked her, slowly becoming aware that the scent of lavender and jasmine were subtly registering within the interior of the vehicle.

Greer chose her words slowly. The terrain before her could become uncomfortable territory at any moment. "The chief felt I was the best for the job because I was the one who'd studied Munro's habits and because..."

Her voice drifted off as she searched for the right way to say this. The least hurtful way to say this.

This time, the momentary silence made him uneasy. "Yes?"

Greer slanted a quick glance in his direction. Could it really be that Kincannon didn't remember her? He seemed far too sharp for that, but maybe he'd blocked it all out. Not all survival mechanisms kicked in on conscious levels.

She took a breath and then continued. "Because you and I have a history."

She'd said the last part softly as she drove away from the courthouse. Slowing down, she slanted another glance toward the judge to see if there was any sign that he knew what she was referring to. His expression remained identical to the one he'd worn a few moments ago.

"A history," Kincannon repeated. There was neither feeling nor a quizzical note evident in his voice. She had no clue if he did actually recognize her.

Okay, she supposed she had to ask, although, in asking, she was aware that she was bringing it all up for him again. Part of her really didn't want to do that. She hated seeing anyone in pain. But as long as she felt in the dark as to whether or not the judge remembered that she was the one who'd been first on the scene of his wife's fatal accident, she was going to constantly feel as if she was walking on eggshells, afraid of the information coming out at the wrong time.

It was a Band-Aid she had to pull off. Now.

"Is that what they call it these days?" Kincannon finally commented.

She took a breath. This time his voice said everything she needed to know. "Then you remember."

He looked at her for a long moment, the events of that dark day coming at him like a lethal assault on all fronts.

He could never think of that day without bitterly tasting the loss. He and Margaret were just coming back from dinner. It was their second anniversary and he couldn't wait to get her home. Couldn't wait to make love with her and count his blessings that he had found his soul mate so early in his life.

He never got to do either.

"That you were the one who cut my seat belt and dragged me out of the car wreck? That you worked over my wife for fifteen minutes, until the paramedics came? Yes, I remember."

Greer frowned to herself. How had Kincannon known how long she'd labored over his wife? When she'd finally sat back and silently admitted to herself that death had won, she'd seen that the man she later learned was a sitting judge in her area had slipped into merciful unconsciousness.

Looking at him now, she realized that she was sitting beside a man who made it a point to know as much as he could about everything. "You tracked down the responding paramedics and talked to them, didn't you?"

He nodded. It had cost him to do it. Had cost him even more to listen to the two men recount their own futile efforts to resuscitate his wife, but he'd hoped that if he did, if he knew everything that had been done, the very knowledge would somehow begin to usher in closure for him and he could start to heal.

He was still waiting.

# Chapter 9

A movement at the back of the courtroom caught Blake's attention despite the fact that the defense attorney pacing before the bench was actively questioning a witness.

For just a split second, his focus shifted away from the proceedings and onto the man in the back of the room. Blake felt his heart rate increase enough to be noticeable. It was then that he admitted, if only to himself in the privacy of his own mind, that the shooting incident had actually spooked him.

He'd already been well aware of how tentative life could be. One moment you were here, the next you were gone. Just like that.

His brother had been larger than life with an aura of tremendous energy about him. Scott had embraced life and wanted to do great things. Margaret was the very definition of sunshine, lighting up his life every moment she was in it. Everyone who knew her loved her. And in what amounted to a blink of an eye, they were both gone. Forever.

Even so, there was a part of him that still felt bulletproof. He felt as if he would go on forever, no matter what.

Probably because it no longer meant anything to him. Those who wanted nothing more than to go on living didn't. Those who didn't care one way or another, leaning toward not, went on interminably.

But being fired at the other day had made him jumpy, if only because he didn't like having the unexpected sprung on him. He liked things mapped out, liked knowing what was coming.

Court had been in session for the past three hours and the defense attorney had only begun to cross-examine the witness who was currently seated in the witness box. There was no reason for anyone to enter the courtroom at this point, no sequestered witness being summoned to give his or her testimony.

Yet someone had entered.

That someone was leaning over, saying something to O'Brien. Blake focused and noticed that the man in the gray sports jacket seemed, at least at this distance, to have the same coloring and features as his bodyguard. Except that he had dark hair and O'Brien was a blonde.

Whatever the man had said to her had O'Brien vacating her seat in the last row, where she'd been ever since court had begun today. The next moment, the man slid into the row, taking her place.

Before he could even form the question in his mind, O'Brien left the courtroom.

Had something happened?

Had Munro been caught? Or had whoever decided these things called off the bodyguard detail?

And who the hell was this new player in the back of his courtroom?

Curiosity he didn't think he possessed anymore rose to bedevil Blake. He wasn't going to get any answers now, not unless he called a halt to the proceedings and inconvenienced everyone but himself.

His curiosity would keep.

Blake forced himself to focus on what was going on in front of his bench. That was, after all, what they were paying him for.

The moment Blake brought his gavel down, declaring recess for lunch, he was on his feet. But rather than retreat to his chambers as was his habit, he stepped down from behind his desk and crossed to the back of the room. He had questions.

The man he wanted to question was coming right toward him. The closer the man came, the more Blake thought that he bore a striking resemblance to O'Brien. One of the Cavanaughs?

And then it hit him a split second before the man reached him.

"You're one of her brothers, aren't you?"

Humor quirked Ethan's mouth as he pretended to

look down at himself. "Does it show? I thought I hid the battle scars pretty well."

The other man was cracking jokes. Blake had his answer. "That would make you Ethan."

The amused smile widened. "That it would, Your Honor. What gave me away?" he asked, curious. A lot of people who knew them managed to confuse him with his brother and the judge was a complete stranger.

"You're smiling," Blake answered. "Detective O'Brien said that your brother Kyle was the more somber one."

"Not anymore," Ethan confided with genuine pleasure. "Kyle's been smiling a lot lately. Mostly due to Jaren," he added. "Jaren Rosetti is another detective on the force. Homicide."

This was far more information than he needed or wanted, Blake thought. What was it about the O'Briens—or the Cavanaughs for that matter—that seemed to compel them to feel that they were somehow responsible for maintaining the mental well-being of the world at large?

"Why are you here, Detective? And where's your sister?" For half a second, hope flashed through him. But then, oddly enough, it was followed by a strange hollowness. He instantly dismissed it, attributing the feeling to the fact that he was hungry. "Am I to assume by her absence that she's not required to hover around me any longer?"

"Sorry to be the one to tell you, but Greer'll be hovering for a while longer. I'm just here to spell her so that she can go home, pack a few changes of clothing and tie up a few loose ends. Specifically one important one."

He knew he shouldn't ask, knew he shouldn't care. Whatever the woman was up to didn't concern him. Except that he was curious.

Blake didn't have a clue where all this curiosity was suddenly coming from, but it prompted him to ask, "What sort of loose ends?"

All around them, people were emptying out the courtroom. Ethan stepped to one side to get out of the assistant district attorney's way. He offered the woman a quick smile. It was a purely ingrained reflexive action, brought on whenever he was in the proximity of an attractive woman.

"Greer needs to find someone to take care of Hussy for her." He chuckled softly. "Doesn't trust either me or Kyle to do it."

The name meant nothing to him. Did it refer to a car—he knew people who named their cars. A child? A cat? "What's a hussy?"

Ethan struggled not to laugh. "You're lucky you asked me and not Greer because that's a straight line she wouldn't be able to resist," he told the judge.

"Lucky," Blake repeated with absolutely no feeling. "So enlighten me."

The bailiff who had been sent in to fill the vacancy left by Tim Kelly's murder looked toward him, a silent question in his eyes. Blake nodded, giving the man permission to leave.

"Hussy is the dog my sister rescued," Ethan was saying.

"From a shelter?" Blake asked even as he told himself he really didn't care to be inundated with details about her life away from the job. What difference did it make to him where the animal had come from? Yet he was curious.

"From two coyotes that had decided Hussy would make an adequate breakfast. Skinniest thing you ever saw when Greer brought her home. She had to work really hard to get that dog to trust her."

Their eyes met and Blake couldn't shake the feeling that O'Brien's brother was telling him more than his words suggested.

"You should see Hussy now. Doesn't even *look* like the same animal. Don't tell her I said so, but Kyle and I think Greer's got a gift," Ethan said, lowering his voice. "She 'loves' things back to health."

What was that supposed to mean?

For that matter, Blake suspected he was having his leg pulled. The story didn't ring true. "Just what does a slip of a woman do to scare off two coyotes?" he wanted to know. The stories he'd heard made a point of the fact that of late, driven by hunger, coyotes were getting pretty brazen in the early morning light.

"Something'll get lost in the translation if I explain. You should ask her to show you sometime."

*Not likely.* Blake made a disparaging noise under his breath. He was in no need for an installment of show-and-tell. "I'll be going to my chambers to have lunch," he informed this newest Detective O'Brien he had to deal with.

Ethan nodded amiably, gesturing for him to go first. "Lead the way, Your Honor."

Blake remained where he was. Security had been doubled. A rat with a hip replacement couldn't sneak by the metal detector, much less a gun-wielding drug dealer. Just what did this O'Brien think was going to happen if he went to his chambers for some much-needed solitude?

"I'd prefer to have it alone," he informed the detective.

"I'm sure you would," Ethan responded cheerfully. "And I feel for you, Judge, I really do. But the chief'll have my head if I don't hang around you—and so would Greer." He inclined his head toward the other man just a little. "And to tell you the truth, she scares me a lot more than the chief does. Greer doesn't pull her punches," he confided.

There was just no winning, Blake thought with exasperation. Turning on his heel, he motioned for the other man to follow him to his chambers.

Greer didn't stop to catch her breath until she was in her car again, on her way back to the courtroom. She'd spent the past hour practically running from place to place, trying to get everything done in as short amount of time as possible.

There was a duffel bag in the trunk, stuffed with everything she'd need for a week's stay just in case this little detail she was shackled to dragged on and she didn't get a chance to get back to her place. She'd arranged for her next-door neighbor, Mrs. Rosenbloom, to pick up her mail. She knew the retired junior high school English teacher would like nothing better than to have an actual excuse to go through her mail.

The sprinklers were programmed on a timer set to go off every other day so that she wouldn't return to a dead lawn. Most important, she'd made arrangements for Hussy to stay with Patience. Her half sister was only one of two within the Cavanaugh clan who wasn't directly in law enforcement. Janelle was the other. The latter had thrown her lot in with the court system while Patience, bless her, was a veterinarian. More than that, she was a vet with just the right kind of touch.

Hussy, poor baby, tended to be a huge chicken when it came to being handled by anyone but her. Some in-depth investigative work on her part had uncovered that Hussy's former owner had abused her, using the small mongrel dog as a training tool for the pit bulls he was breeding. That was why the poor thing was missing part of her ear.

Skittish around people she didn't know, Hussy had nonetheless taken to Patience right from the start. Which was why she'd decided to leave Hussy with the woman instead of asking one of her brothers to swing by her house once a night to feed the dog and let her out in the yard.

Patience had been more than happy to look after the dog. And she wasn't housing Hussy in one of the runs at the animal hospital where other dogs whose masters were away were boarded. Instead, Patience told her that she was going to take the dog home with her.

Greer could have sworn that Hussy had smiled when she'd handed the leash over to Patience.

With her mind at ease, Greer felt she could give the proper amount of undivided attention to her assignment: making sure that Judge Blake Kincannon remained unharmed.

Her mouth curved slightly. She was sure that was going to just thrill the man. Not that she could really blame him. Being independent herself, she could certainly understand Kincannon's resistance to the situation. He was caught between a rock and a hard place. Refusing left him unprotected. No one liked feeling vulnerable, as if they had a target painted on their forehead. But men like Kincannon didn't like being forced to obey rules that were not of their own making, didn't like feeling hemmed in and trapped. Didn't like their every move being watched and shadowed.

The judge gave her the impression that he'd always shouldered his way through life. He was a protector, if she didn't miss her guess, not a protectee.

She felt for him. That didn't mean that she was going to let him have his way. She was here for however long the chief felt she should be.

*Sorry, Judge. Sometimes we just have to play the hand we're dealt,* she thought as she pulled into the courthouse parking lot. It was only half full, which meant that people were still out to lunch.

Her own lunch was sitting in a bag next to her on the passenger seat. Three different kinds of meat mated with two different cheeses and then drizzled with oil and vinegar before being stuffed into twelve inches of crusty French bread.

At the rate she ate, she figured it would be her lunch and possibly her dinner, as well. Dinner for Kincannon and his father was going to be something she'd put together once she brought the judge home. During her nonstop marathon hour she'd made a point of picking up some groceries. She'd deposited them at the judge's house just after she'd brought Hussy to stay with Patience.

For a few seconds, she debated eating her lunch in the car, then decided that she'd been gone long enough. Ethan was doing her a favor; she didn't want to abuse it. If she did, she knew she wouldn't hear the end of it for a very long time. Ethan had the kind of memory that elephants envied.

Besides, all things being equal, she'd rather be up in Kincannon's chambers than sitting in a hot car.

At the thought of the judge, Greer became aware of a strange feeling rifling through the pit of her stomach, unsettling it. Under different circumstances, she would have called what she felt butterflies, but there was no reason to *have* butterflies. This was just an assignment, no different from any other.

Okay, maybe a little different, but that didn't change the basics. She was a detective acting as a bodyguard. She was definitely not invested in this situation as a woman, only as an agent of the law. There was absolutely no reason for her to feel anything at all except responsible for keeping the man alive.

But there was a part of her that did wish Kincannon wasn't so damn sexy. It made things harder on her.

*Doesn't matter if the man looks like Johnny Depp in one of his better roles,* she upbraided herself. *Blake Kincannon is just an assignment, not a man.*

Right. And she was a turnip, Greer thought as she entered the courthouse lobby.

In order for her to get to any of the courtrooms—or even the bathroom for that matter—security required that she had to pass through a metal detector and then walk by the scrutinizing eye of a dour-faced policeman. The man made her think of a troll sitting beneath a bridge.

"What's in the bag?" the policeman fairly growled the question as he watched her place both of her weapons and her cell phone on the conveyer belt. He looked completely unimpressed when she flashed her shield at him. He was programmed to do a job and *nothing* was going to get in his way.

"A sandwich," she responded cheerfully. To prove it, she crossed to him and opened the bag so that he could verify the contents for himself.

The policeman, Officer DeVry, muttered something under his breath and waved her on. As she picked her weapons and cell phone up on the other side of the screening apparatus, Greer heard what sounded like his stomach rumbling audibly.

Greer raised her eyebrows as she looked in the officer's direction. "Hungry?" she asked.

"Yeah," he grumbled.

She'd always been good at small talk. It was a tool

to get people to relax around her. "When's your lunch break?"

"Not for a while," he complained. "They're short-handed because of the shooting and I can't go get anything for another ninety minutes."

Greer thought for a moment. Most likely, she was going to be dealing with this man for at least the next week if not longer. Having him view her in a friendly frame of mind might come in handy.

Taking the sandwich out of the bag, she separated the two halves. They'd already been cut by the boy behind the counter who'd built the sandwich for her.

Dropping one half back into the bag, Greer held the other half out to the officer like a peace offering. "Here."

DeVry eyed the offering suspiciously, making no move to take it from her.

"Here what?" he wanted to know.

The officer was sitting in a chair that had an arm extension on it. She placed the half she'd offered him on the extension.

"I'd take it as a personal favor if you had this half. I hate wasting food and there's just too much here for me to finish. Take it off my hands, Officer DeVry?"

With that, Greer turned on her heel and hurried over to the escalator before the bewildered officer could say anything.

She heard wrapping paper being quickly disposed of as the escalator took her up to the next floor. Greer smiled to herself.

Judge Kincannon's courtroom was empty when she

walked in. It looked as if court was still in recess, she thought.

Crossing the length of the room, Greer circumvented the judge's desk and went through the door on the left that led to the hall and to Kincannon's chambers. That door was closed, as well. She knocked on it once.

Not waiting for a response, Greer turned the doorknob and walked in.

Kincannon was at his desk, reviewing something that had him frowning to himself.

*Nothing new there,* she thought.

Her brother was on the leather sofa, reading a paperback book that he'd stuffed into his pocket earlier when she'd asked him to stay with the judge for an hour. Most likely he was reading a play, she guessed. Ethan had a weakness for theater productions. Being in them, not seeing them. Ethan was the family ham.

"Hi, I'm back," she announced just as Kincannon looked up. Tongue in cheek, she asked, "Did you miss me?"

"What I realized," Kincannon answered, "was that I'd missed the silence. In the past twenty-four hours, I haven't had any."

Rather than rise to the bait, she glossed right over it. "Ethan's not that much of a talker," she agreed, setting down the bag that now only contained half a sandwich.

Both Blake and Ethan laughed shortly, the sound merging. Just like when both her brothers used to gang up on her when they were growing up. She liked to point out that it took two of them to equal one of her.

"Compared to you, an auctioneer isn't much of a talker, either," Blake told her.

He wasn't fooling her, she thought. Her eyes crinkled as she drew her conclusion. The man *had* missed her. The fact that he would probably go to his grave rather than admit it didn't matter.

"Thanks for filling in," she told her brother. "You can go back to your homicide now."

Kincannon looked mildly interested. "She always boss everyone around?" he asked Ethan.

"For as long as I can remember, Judge. Good luck," he addressed the remark to Kincannon, not Greer. "And I mean that from the bottom of my heart."

"He means he would if he had one," Greer corrected.

Blake said nothing. He was too caught up in re-membering. Scottie and he used to engage in the same kind of banter. It reminded him how much he missed his younger brother.

"See you later, Greer." And then Ethan nodded at him. "Goodbye, Judge, nice meeting you."

"Goodbye," Blake murmured, already turning his attention back to what he was doing. And trying very hard not to notice that the woman had the crisp, fresh smell of the wind about her.

It seemed rather appropriate, he couldn't help thinking, seeing as how Detective Greer O'Brien had all but blown into his life.

# Chapter 10

"So, what are we having tonight?" Alexander asked, seeming to materialize at the door the moment that Greer opened it.

Tired, Greer still grinned as she dropped her shoulder bag on the hall table and removed her weapon, still in its holster. She placed it next to her purse. Her secondary weapon she only removed when she was going to bed.

It was a little more than three weeks into her assignment and she and the senior Kincannon had hit a comfortable stride.

After what seemed like several initial false starts, she sensed that the former gunnery sergeant had begun to view her as the daughter he'd never had. His own wife had died years ago and, from what he'd told her, he'd never really gotten to know his late daughter-in-law. He, Margaret and his son would get together around the holidays, but only if he was stationed in the area, which wasn't very often.

Alexander now called her by her first name rather than by her last and things were now comfortable between them. Greer wished she could say the same for her and the judge. Though he didn't say it in so many words, Kincannon still looked as if he would rather she wasn't around, which made her job more difficult.

"In the interest of time," she said in answer to Alexander's question about dinner, "I was thinking of making shrimp alfredo."

Greer knew that she, like all the other Cavanaughs, had a standing invitation to drop by Andrew's anytime for a meal. She'd done it the first night because she needed something to break the ice, but left to her own devices, she liked cooking and there was something very intimate and bonding about cooking for these two bachelors.

Widowers, she silently corrected herself. Both men had loved and lost in the cruelest way nature could devise, long outliving the women they had vowed to love, honor and cherish to the end of their days.

At least they'd loved someone, she thought wistfully, which was more than she could say. Of course, it was hard to fall in love when you kept a tight rein on your heart the way she did. But she was determined not to be hurt the way her mother had been and the only way to prevent it was not to fall in love in the first place.

"Sounds good to me," the older Kincannon enthused. "I'm partial to seafood," he said, telling her something she'd already found out for herself. "Need any help?"

The offer, out of the blue, surprised her. Her eyes crinkled as she told the man, "I could use some company. You up for that, Gunny?"

"Sounds like something I can handle," Alexander told her amiably as he slid onto a stool by the counter. He watched her gather the ingredients that another detective had dropped off earlier. "You know, this isn't so bad, having a woman around."

She knew that as far as former gunnery sergeant Alexander Kincannon was concerned, he'd just given her a very high compliment. When she'd first arrived, Greer was well aware that the older man resented her intrusion into the home he shared with his son almost as much as his son did. Added to that was the fact that he didn't feel that women belonged in law enforcement doing anything other than sitting behind a desk. With all of that stacked up against her, things could have become a little dicey.

But they didn't.

"Wish your son felt that way," Greer said offhandedly as she separated the already cooked shrimp from their tails. She threw the shrimp, one by one, into a bowl and the shells surrounding their tails onto a paper towel.

"He minds less than he lets on," Alexander assured her. "Blake just has trouble letting his feelings show. He's used to keeping everything all bottled up."

She raised her eyes to the man sitting opposite her, barely able to suppress her smile. "Gee, I wonder where he got that from."

Alexander shook his head. "Beats me."

What really amused Greer was that Blake's father

was being serious. He didn't see the connection of his passing on his behavior to his son.

A noise behind him had Alexander swiveling his seat to the right to get a better look. Blake had just walked into the kitchen.

"Speak of the devil," Alexander marveled, chuckling under his breath. "Hey, Blake, we were just talking about you."

Blake stopped short of the refrigerator and the cold drink that had been his goal. Suspicion flittered across his features as he looked from his father to the woman who, unbeknownst to her, was increasingly getting under his skin.

"Why?"

Greer decided to answer before his father said anything to get her in trouble. There was no telling how the older man would deliver the truth.

"Your father seems comfortable having me around. I just commented that I wish you felt the same way."

Opening the refrigerator and taking out a can of soda, Blake popped the top. He took a drink, nudging the refrigerator door closed with his elbow. His eyes shifted toward her before he said anything.

"Hard to feel comfortable with someone shadowing my every step." He took another long sip and then laughed shortly. "I guess I should count myself lucky you let me use the bathroom by myself, without requiring me to share the experience."

Alexander's laugh was far less subdued or guarded. "Might prove interesting," he commented more to himself than to either one of them.

Blake sighed. He knew better than to take his father to task for making the comment. The odds were fifty percent against him that Gunny might say something even worse the next go-round.

So instead, Blake nodded at the pot that was growing crowded with shelled shrimp. "That dinner?"

"It will be," she answered.

Kincannon didn't usually come out of his office until dinner was ready. She'd learned in the first few days that the judge was a man of routines. That was good for her when it came to keeping tabs on him, but not so good when it came to the matter of the lowlife who was after him. A routine was something they could easily use to their advantage.

*That's what you're here for, remember?* she reminded herself. It was up to her—and the patrolmen who periodically drove by Kincannon's house—to keep the judge safe even within his routine.

"Something on your mind, Judge?" she asked mildly, filling a second pot with water and placing it on the front burner. A sealed box of angel hair pasta lay on the counter beside the stove burners.

He took a breath, as if silently saying *now or never.* "What are my chances of getting a furlong?"

She went on working, even as she raised her eyes to his face. She couldn't gauge what he was thinking. "From work or from me?"

He never hesitated. But he did, she thought, smile just the smallest bit. What was *that* all about? "The latter."

*Dream on, Judge. It's just* not *going to happen.*

"About a million to one." Greer raised her eyes to his

just for a fleeting moment. "Possibly even greater than that."

It was no more than he apparently expected. "That's what I thought," he replied with a nod. "I'll just tell them no."

Now he had her curious. Greer adjusted the temperature under the pot. "Tell who no?" she wanted to know.

Blake hesitated for a moment, debating just answering her question with a careless shrug as he left the room. But he knew her rather well by now. Greer wouldn't stop until she found out what he was referring to.

So he told her and saved them both a lot of needless interaction. "Aurora Memorial Hospital is having one of their fundraisers. They're trying to raise enough money to build a new leukemia wing."

"Worthy cause," she commented. Greer's voice was low, but there was no mistaking the genuineness of her feelings.

That surprised him. He thought the police force was only into pushing their own charities to the exclusion of all else. Apparently there were exceptions.

"Yes, it is," he agreed. "They asked me if I would say a few words to jump-start the donations, get them flowing."

She was still waiting for him to come to the heart of his dilemma. When he didn't, she prodded him. "So far, I don't see a problem."

Blake looked at her, his eyes meeting hers. "You, Detective, you're the problem."

In the middle of purloining a shrimp out of the bowl

to sneak a taste, Alexander sprang to her defense. "Hey, go easy on her, Blake."

Greer held up her hand for a moment, stilling her silver-haired protector. "That's okay, Gunny. My fault. I did ask."

The water began to boil and she slid out half the spaghetti in the box. The next moment, she'd removed the pot's lid, broke the spaghetti in half and rained it into the pot. She did the same with the second half.

Only then did she glance at Kincannon over her shoulder. "You're afraid I'll embarrass you?" she asked in a mild tone, as if they were merely discussing the weather.

It wasn't her but the situation that embarrassed him. "Most judges don't have bodyguards."

"Most judges didn't receive a threat on their lives and their family's lives via their personal laptop," she pointed out. Greer dusted her hands on the makeshift apron she'd tied on.

"If they do have bodyguards, those bodyguards *look* like bodyguards." And that, he concluded, made his argument for him.

Stirring the spaghetti, Greer turned her attention back to the shrimp. The judge's father had already disposed of four and was working on a fifth. Melting butter and garlic in the frying pan, she tossed in the shrimp that had escaped Alexander's questing fingers and began to stir.

"I could ask my brother to go with you," she speculated, "although he probably doesn't look burly enough to suit your purposes, either." Chewing on her lower lip, she considered the situation. "Or, I could just go disguised," she told him brightly.

"You mean as one of the hostesses serving drinks or appetizers?" He supposed that might work.

He was in no way prepared for what she was about to say next.

"No, as your date."

He looked at her, the words not registering. "Excuse me?"

Turning down the heat, Greer rested the stirring spoon on a plate since there apparently was no spoon rest. "I'm assuming that invitees are allowed to bring along a guest. Am I wrong?"

Hope had sprung eternal—for exactly three seconds before it had sunk to an ignoble death. "No, you're not wrong."

To her it was the perfect solution. "Okay, then it's all settled. You get to go to the fundraiser. Nobody has to know that I'm guarding you." The spaghetti was ready. She turned off the heat and began to look for a strainer.

"I'll know."

Instead of allowing herself to get deeper into a discussion where she apparently had the opposing view, Greer merely smiled.

"That, Judge, is the whole point. Knowing your back is covered so that you can relax."

A quick search through the cabinets told her that there was no colander. These people really *didn't* do any cooking at home, did they? she thought.

"Having you around has the exact opposite effect."

She put her seemingly futile search on hold and turned around to look at Kincannon. "Did you just give me a compliment, Judge?"

He had, but he hadn't meant to. "I'll be in my office," he told her abruptly, turning on his heel. "Tell me when dinner's ready."

Taking two towels—they didn't seem to have pot-holders, either—she picked up the pot with the spaghetti and slid the lid back only a fraction in order to drain out the water. Even so, she never missed a step and answered, "Will do, Your Honor."

The amusement in her voice followed him all the way down the hall.

Blake straightened his bowtie, looking at the reflection in his wardrobe mirror to get it right.

He had his doubts about this, about attending the fundraiser at all with Munro and his henchmen still on the loose out there. Fairly confident that nothing would happen to him in a ballroom full of people, there was still a very small part of him that worried. Not for himself, but for any innocent bystander who might get hurt if Munro did materialize to make an attempt on his life.

And as for having to go with a bodyguard, that still irritated him. He had no desire to have others think he was being coddled. It was bad enough that the people at the courthouse knew the details. Word had spread with incredible speed within the judicial community, both about Munro's escape and about the threat that the drug dealer had sent to his laptop. It didn't exactly take a genius to put two and two together and figure out what Detective O'Brien was doing, hanging around in his courtroom day after day.

Or what she was doing, going to this fundraiser as his "date."

Blake was really leaning toward calling the chairwoman of the gala, making his apologies and canceling his appearance when he came down the stairs.

Greer had gotten downstairs ahead of him. He could hear her talking to his father. His0 father had just said something to make her laugh and the sound seemed to almost undulate toward him like the movements of a seductive belly dancer.

He banished the image from his mind.

This was a bad idea, he decided, going with her under this pretext.

He was going to tell her that he wasn't feeling well. She couldn't try to argue him out of that, whereupon it was more than an even bet that if he told her he'd just decided not to go, she'd handcuff him to the interior of the sedan and drive to the hotel where they were holding the fundraiser.

Sick it was, he decided. He raised his voice as he approached the living room. "Detective, I've thought it over and—"

That was when it happened. That was the exact moment that he was hit by a Mack truck.

Or at least that was the way it felt to him. The sight of Greer completely knocked the wind out of him.

With her light blond hair curled and loose around her shoulders, she was wearing a strapless ice-blue gown, the hem just whispering along the floor as she turned away from his father and toward him. The top part—the bodice he thought he'd heard his wife once tell him it was called—seemed to be twinkling. He realized that there were hundreds of sequins responsible for that, for catching the light and flashing it back at him like so many tiny, flirtatious stars.

The rest of her gown, staying as close to her torso as he found himself wishing that he could, hugged her curves. It was only when she walked that he realized there was a slit in the front of her gown that went clear up to her thigh, exposing a near perfect expanse of leg. There was a sudden, almost uncontrollable itch in his fingers. He wanted to touch her.

He felt as if he was coming unglued.

The sensuous—it couldn't be called anything else and still be accurate—smile that greeted him made his insides spasm and tighten as if he'd suddenly received a powerful blow to his stomach.

Greer's eyes swept over him as if she was taking every inch of his six-foot-two-inch frame into consideration. "You clean up nicely, Judge."

"You, too," he heard someone with a deep voice murmuring. It was only after several moments that he realized that the words had come from him.

The smile she gave him in response stole his breath away. Again.

"Thank you," she said.

Alexander seemed amused by the exchange he was witnessing. Or maybe it was just the mesmerized look on his son's face that tickled him.

"You two just going to stand there, gawking at each other, or are you actually going to go to this begging fest?"

"Fundraiser, Dad," Blake corrected him, coming to. "It's a fundraiser."

The snort from Alexander told him that the former gunnery sergeant felt he knew better. "Hey, a rose by any other name…you know."

"Give it a rest, Dad," Blake said, trying to bank down the edge in his voice.

The doorbell rang before Alexander could fire back at his son.

Swinging around, Greer instantly tensed. Her hand flew to the pistol that was holstered high on her inner thigh.

The retrieval had attracted the undivided attention of both men.

"Damn, but you are a beautiful sight, Detective O'Brien," Alexander murmured under his breath, his eyes all but glued to the length of her exposed leg. "And I should be twenty years younger."

If she heard the senior Kincannon's declaration, she gave no indication. Her attention was completely focused on the front door and whoever was standing on the doorstep. Her partner was coming to stay with Blake's father while the judge and she attended the fundraiser, but that didn't mean that he was the one standing on the other side of the door right now. It could just as easily be one of Munro's people, ringing the bell to throw her off her guard and gain admittance.

Holding her weapon with both hands and aiming it

at the door, Greer approached it slowly. When she was less than five feet away, she called out, "Who is it?"

"The Big Bad Wolf," the deep male voice belonging to the man standing behind the door told her. "Now open up the damn door or I'll huff and I'll puff and I'll blow your door down."

"House," she said, relaxing. Lowering her weapon, Greer holstered it again. This time she was very aware that she had an audience. "Or else I'll blow your *house* down," she corrected her partner as she unlocked the door and opened it. "At least get it right if you're going to quote fairy tales to me."

"Sorry." The apology echoed with sarcasm as Jeff walked in. "I promise to do better next time." Getting his first glimpse of her, her partner stopped in his tracks. He made no attempt to hide the fact that he was staring at her and that he was impressed by what he saw. A low whistle of deep appreciation escaped his lips. "Especially if you promise to wear that dress to work when you finally come back to the office."

Greer laughed, shaking her head. "In your dreams, Carson."

That's where she'd be tonight, Blake thought, realizing that his self-imposed celibacy was disintegrating right before his eyes.

Detective Greer O'Brien was going to be in his dreams.

Looking just like that.

# Chapter 11

Given the present circumstances, Blake hadn't expected to enjoy himself at the fundraiser.

But he did.

The evening actually went far better than he thought it would. Because of her.

After the first hour or so, he even felt himself beginning to relax. The initial tension he'd experienced when he'd arrived left his shoulders.

But even as that happened, a different sort of tension whispered through him, one he had a hard time defining. He had ceased to be concerned about someone pegging Greer for what she was, a law enforcement agent charged with keeping him out of harm's way—a fact that had originally threatened his manhood.

One look at the woman beside him in her present outfit and law enforcement was definitely the *last* description that came to anyone's mind. He was even less concerned that somehow one of the food servers that were mingling unobtrusively with the hospital foundation's invited guests would suddenly pull out a gun and either shoot him or take him prisoner. Those kinds of things took place in movies and in the procedurals that were currently littering the TV airwaves, not in real life. He was fairly certain that Munro had probably done the smart thing and fled the country.

What he was tense about, he realized as he accepted his second scotch on the rocks from the bartender, was the way he felt himself reacting to the woman who was, for all intents and purposes, hermetically sealed to his side as he interacted with various people who were in attendance tonight.

The only time he and Greer were separated, and not by all that much distance, was when he took the podium and gave his short address to the other guests. His speech was about the good work that the hospital did as it continued to maintain its high standard of excellence, year after year.

This was the hospital where, he recalled for the crowd's benefit, he'd woken up to discover that he could no longer check the box marked "married" on any form. Where he was told that his wife was dead. He knew, even before anyone said anything, that the E.R. team had done everything humanly in their power to bring his wife around. But Margaret had died on that stretch of road where the drunk driver had hit them and just kept going.

He asked the audience to dig deep into their pockets

so that Aurora Memorial could always keep their doors opened and could continue to be on the cutting edge of all the modern advancements that the medical world had to offer.

When he stepped away from the podium, applause ringing in his ears, he crossed back to the bar and ordered another scotch and soda.

Greer shadowed his every move.

"Easy, Judge," she whispered in his ear, keeping her voice low so that no one could overhear. The last thing in the world she wanted to do was embarrass him. "That's your third one."

Her breath along his neck created a piercing, seductive warmth that went right through him. It took iron will for Blake not to shiver in response.

Not to kiss her.

"Counting, Greer?" He'd almost slipped and called her "Detective." Not something one called their date unless they were locked in a bedroom, role playing, the judge mused.

"Just looking out for you," she said with a smile. "I surmise that you want to maintain the proper, dignified front in public."

Blake deliberately took a long sip from the drink the bartender had passed to him to show Greer that he was his own person and if he set the glass down—which he did—it was by his own choice, not because she'd subtly suggested that he do it.

Turning to face her, he was struck again by how beautiful she looked. And by how attracted to her he was. Since they were in a crowded ballroom, he decided he was safe.

"Do you like dancing, Greer?"

The smile that curved her lips looked incredibly sensual and seductive. He felt himself responding to a degree he had no longer thought possible. "In general or specifically?"

Her question amused him. Maybe he *had* consumed a bit much too quickly, he decided.

The next moment he dismissed the thought. What he was feeling, Blake told himself, was the effect of being here with all those traumatic memories. Not to mention the effect of being here with this woman. The combination was troubling and he'd resorted to what he used to do in college: soak whatever was bothering him in alcohol.

Unconsciously, he pushed the glass on the bar even farther away. "Both," he told her.

"Yes—to both," Greer replied, her eyes meeting his.

He felt something undulate in his stomach. Ignoring it, Blake took her hand and wove his way to the space within the ballroom that had been set aside as a dance floor.

Reaching it, he turned around and took one of her hands, tucking it in his and holding it against his chest while he slipped his other hand around her waist. He caught himself thinking that the woman felt smaller than the image that she projected. Her waist bordered on being tiny.

The tempo was soft, slow, a melodic old show tune

from the forties, and they swayed in time to the melody. Her head was on his shoulder and Blake found himself inhaling the scent that drifted to him from her hair. Something sweet and yet arousing. He could feel his gut tightening again along with a muted anticipation awakening within his body. He tried to bank it down, but he wasn't quite fast enough.

Greer tilted back her head to look at his face. "You dance well."

"I'm a bit rusty," he allowed. "I haven't danced since— I haven't danced," he repeated, abruptly terminating the sentence.

She had a feeling he was going to say he hadn't danced since the last time he'd done it with his wife. Greer had no desire to dig up old wounds so she didn't press for him to continue.

Instead, she nodded amiably. "Some things you don't forget no matter how much time passes. Like riding a bicycle, or dancing. Or making love."

And if she were tortured from now until the apocalypse, she wouldn't have been able to say where that last statement had come from or how it had found its way to her lips. All she could do was pretend she wasn't as stunned by it as he appeared to be.

In an effort to divert his attention, she just continued talking. "Do you like Cole Porter?"

He stared at her as if he believed that she was a collection of non sequitur statements. "Excuse me?"

"Cole Porter," she repeated. "They're playing 'When They Begin The Beguine.' It's a song by Cole Porter. At least I think it's Cole Porter. Or maybe it's by Jerome

Kern. He did the music for *Show Boat*. It's an old musical," she added when he looked at her quizzically. "I have trouble remembering which was which."

Blake laughed shortly. "I'm afraid I can't help you there. All I know about music is whether or not I like it."

"And do you?" she asked softly, turning her face up to his.

Blake felt a wave of heat that had nothing to do with the ballroom's air-conditioning system. It accompanied the sudden, unexpected dryness in his mouth. "Do I what?"

"Like it?" Her voice was husky, barely above a whisper.

"Very much," he replied. "Even if I have no idea what a 'Beguine,' is."

"It's a ballroom dance that was popular back then. I used to watch a lot of old movies on TV as a kid," she explained in case he wondered why she'd know an obscure fact like that.

Her breath was backing up in her lungs. Dancing had nothing to do with it. The man with her did. There were all sorts of feelings skittering through her that left her in a tailspin.

There it was again, she thought helplessly, that feeling that had popped up when she'd thrown herself on top of Blake in the courtroom.

Except that this time, it was bigger, more defined and definitely more forceful.

The applause around them registered abruptly and

he realized that couples were applauding because the music had stopped.

At least, the music that was coming from the band's instruments had stopped. The other music, the melody that seemed to have materialized in his head, was still playing. It took effort not to move to it. Effort not to respond to the raw, unguarded look in Greer's eyes when she slanted a look in his direction.

He had a feeling that she didn't know he'd seen her expression and he was relieved that they were out in public. Because in a moment like this, if they were alone, he might have been tempted to do something completely against his nature. Something completely outside the box.

Clearing his throat, he looked for something to say. "I've been meaning to ask you…your brother said you saved your dog by chasing away a couple of coyotes. He was kidding, right?"

"No, he wasn't," she murmured.

"How?" was all he could ask.

"Coyotes don't like loud, unexpected noises. I raised my hand over my head to seem bigger than I was and growled as loud as I could. They ran," she concluded with a smile that dared him to contradict her.

"And you did this because it just came to you?" he asked skeptically.

She laughed then and he caught himself thinking again how much that sounded like music to him. "Because I watch the Discovery Channel," she corrected. "You can pick up a lot of useful information there."

He wondered if they had a program devoted to surviving exposure to seductive bodyguards.

The fundraiser lasted a total of five and a half hours. After about four and a half, the crowd began to slowly diminish as people started making their excuses and slipping away, either to go home, or to grab a nightcap with a few intimate friends.

The judge, Greer noted, looked as if he was prepared to remain to the bitter end. Curious, she still didn't question him as to whether or not he was obligated to remain at the function, or if he merely wanted to. Hers wasn't to ask why, hers was just to protect unconditionally.

Remaining constantly alert, even as she absorbed the exceedingly positive vibrations coming from the man she was guarding, was taking a toll on her. But she couldn't put her guard down. Danger could come from any one of an endless number of directions.

There were a lot of people in here, people that someone on the fundraising committee could supposedly vouch for. However, the attending guests, not to mention the people catering the affair, were all scattered about like so many marbles. Rounding them all up to verify that they were exactly who they said they were and checking into their background would have taken far too much time. The fundraiser would long be over before she was even half finished.

She had to rely on her gut—and on luck.

When the judge finally shook his last hand and told her that they were going home, Greer could have cheered. Not that she minded being with him like this. Kincannon looked incredibly dynamic in his tuxedo. With hair the color of the inside of midnight and eyes a dark fathomless blue, he easily made her pulse accelerate. But keeping an eye out for anything out of the ordinary, any person who got too close to him, *was* exceedingly wearying.

Heading toward the door with the judge, she struggled to curb her enthusiasm. It took a great deal of effort not to just herd the man out of the building. As it was, she slipped her arm through his and walked faster. He had no choice but to keep up.

"I'll let you drive," Kincannon told her once the valet had brought up his new car and had hopped out of it. When she looked at him quizzically, he explained, "The last thing I want is to be pulled over by some overzealous motorcycle cop and wind up failing a breathalyzer test." Drinking was something he *always* kept under control. The specter of what had happened to his wife was forever with him and he was determined that no other family would *ever* be put through that sort of pain because of him.

She had no problem driving them home. The only beverage she'd consumed all evening was ginger ale. But the fact that he thought he'd consumed more than the acceptable amount of alcohol bothered her. It meant that she'd slipped up in watching him.

"Just how many scotch on the rocks did you have?" she asked as she slid in behind the steering wheel of the silver two-seater.

Getting in on the passenger side, Blake buckled up. "Three."

Three drinks over the space of the evening didn't seem like much and he didn't sound like a man who was even mildly inebriated. However she saw no reason to argue and she did like driving his vehicle. This was probably the closest she would ever come to driving a Mercedes sports car.

Still, she did want him to know that she thought he was perfectly fit. "You seem very sober to me."

Kincannon chuckled. "Hence the saying."

Greer glanced at him as she flew down the road. Traffic seemed to be nonexistent and the lights all seemed to be cooperating, turning green two beats before she reached the intersections.

"Saying?" she questioned.

"Sober as a judge," he replied, an amused smile flirting with his lips.

Okay, maybe Kincannon was a wee bit tipsy, she thought, revising her assessment. It was better to be safe than sorry.

"Good saying," she murmured, her mouth curving.

"I don't know," he countered slowly, as if he was rolling it over in his mind. "It brings an image of a dour-faced, stern individual to mind," he confessed. "Not the professional image I'm going for." He paused, thinking, then put the question to her. "What does fair and impartial look like?"

She slanted a glance at him. The moment he asked, the answer came to her. "Like you."

Silence slipped in and accompanied them the rest of

the short distance home. For once, she did nothing to break it. But she did notice that though he might have been embarrassed by her honesty, there still was the barest hint of a smile on his lips.

Detective Jeff Carson left the judge's house less than five minutes after they arrived. The older Kincannon, her partner told them as he struggled to suppress a yawn, had gone to bed over an hour ago. Beyond that, he had nothing to report, other than Gunny had taken him in poker, winning eight hands out of ten.

"I should have warned you about that," Blake confessed. "He's practically a card shark, a side effect of being posted in out-of-the-way places where they roll the sidewalks up at night." He reached for his wallet, obviously intending to make up for what her partner had lost.

Greer put her hand on his, stopping him from taking the wallet out. "Carson's a big boy, aren't you, Carson? No one forced him to play poker with your father."

"Big boy," Jeff echoed none-too-happily as he left. "G'night."

"Good night, Jeff." Greer closed the door, securing it. Crossing back to the sofa, she sank down with a huge sigh. "I'm going to change—as soon as I get the energy to get up again."

Blake looked at the sofa, shaking his head. He still didn't like the idea of Greer sleeping on it. "You know, you can use one of the guest rooms," he prompted.

She shrugged carelessly. Though she didn't use a guest room at night, she still had her clothes stashed in the one closest to the staircase. "I've gotten to like sleeping on the sofa."

He paused, scrutinizing her. "You lie as smoothly as you tell the truth."

Greer grinned, not bothering to dispute his assessment. "You pick things up along the way. Good night, Judge," she said, hoping that would send him on his way. It was late.

He needed to put distance between them. In his present state, she represented far too much temptation. Nodding, Blake murmured, "Good night." He was on his way out of the room, heading toward the staircase, when he stopped.

He had no idea why he stopped.

Maybe it was a need to unburden himself to this woman who seemed to coax words out of him so easily. Maybe the memory of their one intimate dance was still fresh on his mind, threatening to forever imbed itself into his memory. He couldn't be sure.

All he did know was that he remained standing where he was, staring at the staircase, telling Greer what he had never told anyone before.

"She wanted children, you know." He turned around to face Greer. "Margaret, she wanted children."

Greer stiffened ever so slightly, wondering if she should stop him right here before he wound up pouring out his heart. She instinctively knew he would regret that in the morning, regret telling her about his late wife's dreams.

But maybe the man *needed* to talk and she was, after all, a relative stranger as far as he was concerned.

Someone who would be out of his life soon enough. Until their paths crossed again.

Her heart ached for him as she looked at the pain in his eyes.

"No, I didn't," Greer finally replied in a low voice. "I didn't know that."

Blake nodded. Rounding the back of the sofa, he came and sat down beside her. "She did. I talked her into waiting."

She heard the guilt, the sorrow, and knew exactly what he was thinking. He blamed himself that his wife had died never experiencing the love of a child. "You couldn't have known that there was going to be an accident. Or that she would wind up dying. None of us gets to look into the future."

He shook his head. She didn't understand, he thought. Didn't understand because he wasn't clear, he was tripping over his own tongue.

"It wasn't the future, it was the present." Blake blew out a breath. He could see that he had managed to confuse her even more. "She was pregnant," he said with feeling. "The night she was killed, Margaret was pregnant."

Her eyes widened. No one had told her that. Granted she hadn't been involved in the inquiry, or in trying to find the hit-and-run driver who had ultimately wound up running them off the road. She'd just happened to be the off-duty officer who had tried to save two people whose paths she'd crossed.

"Are you sure?" Greer pressed.

He nodded, numb. "That was her big news. She told

me right in the middle of dinner, after I made some inane toast to our second anniversary. She almost burst, holding her secret in. It should have dawned on me when she refused to have a drink before dinner. Having a drink was always part of eating out for her," he explained, remembering.

The judge's face was drawn and Greer could literally see his pain. It was right there, in his eyes. He was struggling not to give in to it, not to let the tears that were shining in his eyes fall.

She was a firm believer in tears, in using them to cleanse away pain, to purge emotions. But men had their own set of codes. Greer had a hunch that shedding tears to relieve tension was just not part of it.

At least not for Blake Kincannon.

But code or no code, there couldn't be anything in his credo that said he was against receiving comfort from another human being. There couldn't be anything against having that other human being put her arms around him and offering him all the silent sympathy that she possibly could.

Which was exactly why Greer put her arms around the man she was supposed to be guarding. Why she held on to him even as Blake initially resisted the contact, trying to pull away. The sofa worked in her favor, foiling him because there was nothing he could do to make her physically back away.

"It takes a strong man to allow himself to be human," she told him in a quiet, firm whisper against his ear. "I'm sorry I couldn't do anything to save her that night," she added.

He'd passed out toward the end, but he'd been there to watch Greer's efforts in the first few minutes. He'd never seen anyone work so hard.

"It wasn't your fault," he told her. He raised his head to look at her. "I don't blame you," he added just in case Greer thought he did. If there was someone to blame, it would be the man driving the car that had hit them. Hit them and then disappeared into the fog that had spread out over the area like a huge cottony spider's web.

"If it wasn't for you, I would have died, too. I owe you my life," he reminded her. His eyes held hers. The attraction he'd felt and fought from the start was all but overwhelming him, pressing against him so hard, he could hardly draw a breath. "I owe you," he whispered, letting his voice faded away.

And then, the next moment, Blake wasn't talking at all.

And neither was she.

A fire had leaped into their veins simultaneously, ignited by feelings too strong to suppress, or to remain dormant and unacknowledged.

Maybe it was the three drinks that eroded his defenses, or maybe they merely made him more in tune to what was happening here. Whatever the reason, Blake sealed his mouth to her lips at the same time that he sealed his soul to hers.

# Chapter 12

Greer prided herself on not being the kind of person who ordinarily lost control, the kind who got carried away if the situation was right.

Labeled by those in authority as a hellion when she was in high school, even then she'd been very much in control of herself, no matter what situation she found herself in. Because she liked to live life fast and hard didn't mean that she ever lost sight of end goals. Never before had she ever even entertained the idea and shouted, "The hell with consequences."

In her mind, she was forever the daughter of an unattached woman who dedicated herself to doing her very best to provide and care for the three children she'd given birth to.

Deep down, Greer was the girl who had been left by her father. Not willingly—she'd believed for more than the first two decades of her life—but the end result was that he was still absent. When she'd heard her mother's deathbed confession that she and her brothers were the product of an affair and that their biological father had deserted them, Greer had settled down and applied herself to becoming an upstanding member of society.

She became a rock.

And, within her heart of hearts, Greer trusted no man implicitly beyond her brothers. Because men left, men abandoned, and she saw the consequences of that. In the back of her mind, residing like an unwanted tenant, was the memory of her mother's socially isolated life. Oh, her mother had been a loving, warm woman who did the best she could but Greer sensed that there was a ragged hole in her mother's heart created by the man who wasn't there. Who'd refused to be there all those years ago.

That was never going to be her, Greer had vowed. And, in order for that to be true, she couldn't allow herself to fall in love with anyone, couldn't go so far into uncharted waters that she lost her way back.

It was a good, solid plan.

So what was she doing here, letting this man with his impossibly sensual mouth kiss her? What was she doing, kissing him back?

And wanting so much more.

Damn it, this wasn't the route to self-preservation. This was the way to self-destruction, the way to lose not just the battle, but the war.

And yet, even though her mind fairly shouted for her to abort her present behavior, to get out now before she slipped any further into the emotional quicksand she was standing in, Greer couldn't get herself to stop. Couldn't get herself to respond and obey. Or even move an inch away.

All she wanted to do was fan the flames that were blazing within her. Wanted more than she'd ever wanted anything before to experience lovemaking with this man.

Every inch of her body yearned for it, begged for it.

She was crazy, absolutely crazy, Greer thought. Maybe it was the flu, maybe she'd caught a strain that short-circuited the brain, making a person behave completely out of character.

Maybe—

She sucked in her breath, startled, as Blake drew back, creating a space between them that felt as big as a chasm.

Greer pressed her lips together, tasting him. She looked at Blake, trying to focus her thoughts, trying to focus her resolve as well as her line of vision. Most of all, she was trying to squelch this bereft feeling that threatened to swallow her up whole and break her down into little pieces.

Blake was talking to her. His mouth was moving but she wasn't absorbing what he was saying. She concentrated harder.

"We can't do this here," he was saying.

Well, thank God at least one of them had some common sense, she thought, breathing a sigh of both relief and huge, frustrated disappointment. The ache in her body felt almost unmanageable.

"You're right," she told him hoarsely.

Blake was rising to his feet. But rather than tell her good-night, he was taking her hand, coaxing her up off the sofa, as well.

Why?

"Come upstairs with me." It was both a question and a supplication.

Her pulse quickened again. The platform beneath her feet suddenly splintered and gave way, sending her free-falling through space. Greer stared at him. "But I thought you just said we can't do this."

"Here," Blake emphasized, underscoring the one word that counted. The one word she hadn't heard. "I said we can't do this *here*. We're out in the open on the sofa and my father sometimes comes down to get something to drink or eat. He has occasional insomnia," he explained.

There was no way that Blake wanted, at his age, to have his father stumble across him in a compromising situation.

"Oh." Greer took a breath. Her insides were actually trembling. What was up with that? She'd been in life-and-death situations and she'd never reacted like this. "Then you didn't want to stop kissing me."

He moved his head slowly from side to side, negating the mere suggestion.

"I'd sooner stop breathing," he told her honestly. And then her words hit him. Belatedly, he gave a different interpretation to them. "Unless you don't want me to kiss you."

He'd left it up to her, she thought, giving her the impression that he would go along with whatever her decision was.

Didn't it matter to him? Was it all just one and the same to the man? *Heads we make love, tails we don't?*

Greer refused to have this all on her shoulders. She lobbed the ball back into his court. "Do you want to kiss me?"

The sinfully sexy smile that rose to his lips out of nowhere made Greer want to throw her arms around him and seal her mouth to his—as well as several other parts of his anatomy. Even the mere promise of contact generated heat within her.

"I think I just answered that question, Greer." But instead of kissing her again the way she hoped he would, Blake moved his fingers through hers. "Come upstairs with me," he coaxed.

"Upstairs?" Did that sound as dumb as she thought it did?

"To my room," he added softly.

She let herself be drawn.

This, no doubt, was the way the mice felt, responding to the Pied Piper's irresistible music when he played it to lead them out of the town. Everyone knew what happened to them, she thought. They were led into the river to perish.

And yet, she couldn't stop herself, couldn't use the momentary break to regroup and refortify herself.

Couldn't offer up the slightest excuse as to why this shouldn't be happening. She could have cited, at the very least, that it was unprofessional of her to sleep with the very man she was supposed to be guarding.

Sleep.

Who was she kidding? She was praying that her time with Blake wouldn't have anything to do with sleep the entire night.

As if in a dream, Greer went up the stairs with Blake, her entire body heating in anticipation of things she had no business expecting or even hoping for.

She couldn't stop herself.

Blake opened the door to his bedroom, and then, rather than walk in, he abruptly stopped. He glanced down at the threshold. Once it was crossed, there was no turning back. Without a word, he raised his eyes to hers and waited.

Taking a breath, knowing that she should be calling a halt to this and yet felt powerless to do so, Greer stepped across the threshold and thus silently sealed her fate.

Following her, Blake closed the door.

And then they were alone. Alone and very much together.

She became aware of her heart pounding in double time as Blake began to kiss her again, his hands roaming along the curves of her body as if he was attempting to memorize every inch, as if he was familiarizing himself with a brand-new world.

The very thought made her heart pound even harder.

Desire and passion scrambled through him, vying

for possession, for some sort of fulfillment. He'd kept himself in check all this time, not just with Greer, but as far as all women, as well. He wasn't the kind of man who had needs to attend to on a regular basis, whose needs took control of him.

Going through the motions had never appealed to Blake, even before he'd ever met Margaret. To him, some sort of a relationship needed to precede becoming intimate with a woman. The act of lovemaking had to involve more than just body parts. The nebulous entity some people referred to as "the soul" had to be included.

If it wasn't, then everything else was just meaningless.

Right now, a sense of urgency filled him, as if he had to outrace his thoughts, because if they were still filled with images of Margaret and caught up to him, the feeling that he was betraying his late wife would hold him back. And he didn't want to hold back. Not now, not after he'd come so far so quickly. There was something about this woman—this woman out of hundreds of others—that set her apart. Something that spoke to him. That made him feel alive and made him long to remain that way.

Very gently, Blake slid the bodice of the blue gown down to her waist. For a moment, he just drank in the sight of her. And then he tugged on the clingy dress, bring it down to first her hips, then her legs, finally sending the shimmering cloth to the floor.

Greer stood there before him in high heels, wearing

a matching strapless light blue bra and a scrap of lacy blue nylon that doubled as underwear.

Her weapon was still holstered and strapped to her inner thigh.

Damn, he'd never seen anything sexier in his life. Blake brought his mouth down on hers.

He felt her lips curve in a smile against his. If there was something funny about all this, he was missing it.

Greer drew her head back just a fraction, her eyes smiling into his. "I think, in the interest of keeping the gun from going off and keeping you intact, I should take my weapon off."

Blake laughed shortly and nodded, releasing her. "Good idea," he agreed.

She made short work of carefully removing the gun and then placing the gun and holster on Blake's nightstand.

Blake lost no time in reclaiming her. The second she straightened up, he began to shower soft, openmouthed kisses on her shoulders, her collarbone, and then her breasts as he eliminated the lacy strapless bra.

By now, desire hummed through him like a freshly struck tuning fork. Though he wanted to rip it away, Blake was careful to slide the exceedingly thin thong down along her hips so that it joined the pool of shimmering blue material on the floor.

Blake couldn't catch his breath. The woman was incredibly beautiful. Just as beautiful as he knew she would be.

"Your turn," she murmured, her eyes holding his.

Blake looked at her, a puzzled expression on his

face. Rather than verbally answer, Greer immediately began to remove his jacket, his tie, his cummerbund, the brilliant white shirt he wore, as well as his trousers, socks and shoes.

She paused in the middle to admire and skim her hands along a rock-solid abdomen. She'd had a feeling that he had a good body, but she had no idea that it would be *this* bone-melting good. She'd seen professional trainers whose abs, chest and arms didn't look nearly as sculpted.

She had to ask. "When do you work out?" He hadn't gone to a gym on her watch and there was no exercise equipment in the house that she knew of.

He ended the mystery by saying, "Push-ups."

If that was the case, she thought, push-ups were highly underrated.

She separated him from the rest of his clothes in record time. And as she got rid of his shoes, Greer stepped out of her own, kicking them aside.

They were both nude, both vulnerable.

The moment she was finished undressing him, Blake pressed his lips to the hollow of her throat, sending the blood in her veins surging.

Needs began to slam into her. Pleading for attention, for release.

They fell onto the bed, their limbs tangling as the passion between them all but exploded.

Greer moaned, anticipation squeezing her in its grip. With each openmouthed kiss along her torso, she found herself coming closer and closer to a climax. She scrambled toward it, eager, yet afraid that once it found her, once she experienced it and the euphoria it generated began to fade, regret and remorse would swiftly follow.

But she had absolutely no choice in the matter. Her body had taken over and just like that, the sensation seized her, sending her flying over the edge. But rather than plummet to earth, the way she fully expected to, the climax flowered into another one and another after that. The rush was incredible even as it was exhausting.

For just a moment, she thought that she would be in its grip forever and ever.

She had no complaints.

Everywhere Blake's lips and tongue touched, she felt immediate fireworks, fireworks that went off in her very core. She wasn't sure just how long she could hold her own before she became too exhausted to breathe. Slick with sweat, she pulled him to her. Then, rolling her body into his, she managed to reverse their positions, putting herself on top.

Straddling him the way she would a motorcycle, she began to move, swaying her body against his. She saw the look in his eyes, the raw desire, and it excited her beyond all boundaries.

That was how he managed to catch her off guard. Blake surprised her by catching hold of her arms. In one swift, seamless motion, he reversed their positions again and he was the one looking down at her. Every breath he took undulated into her. She never took her eyes off him. This was a side to him she would have never guessed existed.

*Didn't you?* a small voice in her head whispered. She banked it down.

Blake threaded his fingers through hers, then raised her hands above her head as he positioned himself over her. Seductively, he began to move a little at a time, increasing his tempo. She gasped, arching. Inviting.

And then he was inside her and they were one entity, one being with only one desire vibrating between them.

Responding to an inner rhythm, Blake began to move his hips again, at first slowly, then with increasing more urgency. She shadowed his every movement, exciting him as much as he excited her.

And then it was a race, not to outdo but to come together.

When the pinnacle they were mutually striving for was reached, Greer bit down on her lip to keep from screaming out her pleasure.

She was breathless. And so, from the sound of it, was Blake.

It made the euphoria gripping her last longer.

She felt Blake hugging her, felt him tightening his arms around her and holding her closer. For one of the few times in her life, Greer felt protected, as if nothing could reach her, nothing could harm her.

Or her heart.

It was illusion, all illusion, and she knew it, but she clung to it nonetheless. Savored it. And pretended, just for a moment, that it was real. And that it would last for as long as she was alive.

Greer became aware that his ardor was cooling just

a bit. After a moment, he shifted his weight, moving off her and onto his back.

She was surprised that he continued holding her. Surprised and pleased, although she said neither. From her experience, men didn't like to feel crowded and any dialogue after the fact dealing with feelings was a signal for them to flee the scene as quickly as was humanly possible.

"You give this kind of service to everyone you're assigned to guard?" he asked, murmuring the question against her ear.

She was amazed, considering what she'd just experienced, that the feel of his breath along her neck was arousing her again. By all rights, she was more than half dead from exhaustion.

And yet...

He was still waiting for her to respond to what she assumed was a semi-serious question on his part. With a careless shrug, Greer gave him a non-answer. "This is my first bodyguard assignment. I'm playing it by ear and improvising as I go along."

"I see." He strummed his fingertips along her curves, enjoying her. "Very innovative of you."

She couldn't tell by his tone if he was serious or not. "Any complaints?" she asked.

"Can't think of a one." He laughed shortly. "Actually, I can't think. You seem to have short-circuited my brain."

She raised herself into a semi-sitting position, resting her chin on his chest and looking up at him. "Maybe your brain's just resting since it wasn't needed."

"Oh, it was needed," he assured her. "Haven't you heard? The brain is the most sexual organ in the human body."

Tilting her head, she looked at him again, mischief playing on her lips. "I seem to recall hearing something like that, yes. So, you want to put it to the test?" she asked. Before he could answer, she continued, carrying on both sides of the conversation. "You want to *think*, Judge? Or do you want to *do?*" she asked, tilting her head as she waited for him to respond.

Rather than answer her the traditional way, Blake caught the back of her head, pulled her to him and brought her mouth down to his.

The kiss stretched down to the very edges of her soul.

She felt his desire for her resurfacing. Growing hard.

Greer grinned, doing her best to hide her own excitement. She had the answer to her question.

"I have my answer," she murmured against his mouth before she threw herself into round two. And lost herself in him completely.

*Chapter 13*

Sleep was an elusive element in Blake's life. Waking at least twice each night, he hadn't managed to come anywhere close to sleeping straight through the night since Margaret had died. He'd just accepted that this was the way things were, just as he'd accepted that he would never have feelings for another woman again.

He was wrong on both counts.

After making love with Greer a second time, he'd drifted off to sleep and slept through the entire night without waking up once.

Slept so soundly that apparently he hadn't heard Greer leave.

When, still semi-asleep, he'd reached for her, he'd found the other half of his bed empty. The sheets were cool to the touch on her side, which meant that she hadn't just left. She'd been gone a while.

Sitting up, Blake saw that she'd taken her clothes with her. And hung his up neatly, folding his socks and underwear and placing them on top of the bureau while his tuxedo and shirt had been returned to their hangers in his closet.

It was, he thought, as if last night had never happened.

Maybe that was the effect she was after, he thought. Maybe she wanted to physically deny what had transpired between them.

Blake scrubbed his hands over his face. He wasn't sure how he felt about that. He knew that a lot of men would have been relieved not to be held accountable. Not to feel that they were going to be tangled up in a bunch of strings and expectations.

But he wasn't like most men.

Still, if he pretended that nothing had happened, then he wouldn't have to feel as if he'd been unfaithful to the memory of his wife. That was something he'd expected to have weigh heavily on him once the passion and desire had cooled and faded and the lovemaking was in the past. But while he was, for the moment, emotionally on shaky ground, oddly enough, there was no guilt pressing down on him.

Maybe he was still in shock, he speculated, getting up. After all, he'd been fully prepared to face the rest of his life as a single man. Loving someone else wasn't even remotely on his agenda. Once was all he thought anyone could logically hope for.

But apparently, he could be wrong.

He *was* wrong, Blake amended, because last night wouldn't have happened if he hadn't felt something for the woman it was happening with.

Ever since he could remember, he'd always needed something more than just chemistry in order to want to be intimate with a woman, although, he mused with a faint smile as he headed off into the shower, there was definitely something to be said for chemistry. Last night had felt as if the whole damn lab had been set on fire and exploded.

As he turned on the water, he concentrated on that and not on the fact that he had let his guard down and allowed the notion of love to creep in.

Less than fifteen minutes later, Blake was dressed and making his way down the stairs. The scent of coffee greeted him when he was less than halfway down.

A man could get used to this, he thought. These past two years he'd forgotten what it was like, coming down to freshly brewed coffee, to the aroma of breakfast being made. Ever since Greer had been assigned to be his bodyguard, coffee and breakfast had suddenly become the norm again.

*Careful, Blake, don't get used to this. She's not a permanent part of your life. Once they catch Munro, she'll be gone.*

He found the thought more than mildly disturbing.

Taking the last step down, Blake could see that Greer was in the living room, folding up the bedding that she'd used. She'd spent the remainder of the night here, he realized.

Why?

"You came down last night?" he asked her, walking into the living room.

It hadn't been her imagination, she thought. She *had* sensed him.

Greer looked at him over her shoulder, doing her best not to flush. She'd left his bed sometime around 1:00 a.m. and come down, but bits and pieces of last night kept replaying themselves in her head until dawn. She'd gotten even less sleep last night than she ordinarily did.

Not knowing how he would react in the light of day after the night they'd shared, she kept her voice neutral. "I'm supposed to be your bodyguard, remember?"

"Couldn't have guarded it more closely than you did last night," he reminded her.

Was that amusement she heard in his voice? And if so, was that a good thing or a bad one?

Greer pressed her lips together. In either case, at least they were addressing the elephant in the living room right off the bat.

She cleared her throat. "About last night…"

He stood where he was, having no idea what to expect next. This was not a run-of-the-mill situation for him. "Yes?"

She forced herself to look into his eyes. "If you want to request another bodyguard, you are within your right to do so."

He stared at her, trying to extract the hidden meaning behind her words. "I don't understand. Why would I want another bodyguard?"

She lifted one shoulder in a shrug. "In case you don't feel comfortable, or…" Her voice trailed off as the words she needed to use deserted her.

He was silent for a moment, and then he smiled.

Slightly. "Looks to me like you're the one who feels uncomfortable."

He was right, Greer thought. She *was* uncomfortable. Uncomfortable with the emotions that he'd aroused within her last night, uncomfortable with how easily she'd capitulated to those emotions. She was usually stronger than that.

Damn it, she should have fought harder to resist him. He didn't strike her as the kind of man who would take advantage of the situation, or of her if she had said no. It had been up to her to stop things before they'd gotten out of hand. Instead, she'd wound up doing everything in her power to speed them along.

"I should have been more in control," she finally told him.

His eyes made her feel that he was looking into her soul, seeing all of her secrets. "There was no pillaging going on," he murmured wryly. "Seems to me that we were equally in control."

Greer read between the lines. Blake obviously thought she was talking about the actual lovemaking. But she wasn't. She was talking about the fact that she shouldn't have allowed last night to have happened in the first place.

The very thought of the night they'd spent together made her pulse begin to accelerate again. Damn it, what was *wrong* with her?

"You're blushing, Detective," Blake pointed out, amused.

She tossed her head, sending her hair flying over her shoulder like a blond shower.

"It's just hot in here." This time, she avoided his eyes. It was safer that way. "I've got to get back into the kitchen and finish making breakfast before the eggs burn," she said, breezing by him and heading toward the kitchen.

Turning on his heel, Blake followed her. "Isn't my father watching them for you?"

"No, I haven't seen your dad yet this morning. He told Jeff last night that he felt tired," she told him, repeating what her partner had said to her before he left. "Maybe he decided to sleep in this morning."

Blake frowned. His father was usually up with the roosters. "That's not like him," he commented. "But then, I wasn't myself either last night."

Entering the kitchen, she slanted a glance at the judge. "Regrets?" she asked, trying her damnedest to sound nonchalant.

"Maybe," he allowed. When she looked at him, he explained further. "That I didn't do it sooner."

She was doing her best to put emotional distance between them, but all the while, she caught herself yearning for an encore of last night. Damn it, was she losing her mind? She didn't behave this way. What had he done to her?

"It has been two years—"

He didn't let her finish. He realized that she didn't understand what he was saying. "That I didn't do it sooner with you," he clarified. He'd felt the sexual pull between them that first day in court, when she'd flown over his desk to shield him.

There went her heart, she thought, feeling it lodge

into her throat. Their eyes met and she caught herself holding her breath.

*Don't buy into this,* she cautioned herself. *It's going to hurt like hell when it's over if you do.*

She knew she was lying to herself. It was going to hurt like hell when it was over no matter what. She was already standing on the threshold of pain.

Greer changed the subject. "Maybe you should go upstairs and see what's keeping your father. Tell him breakfast is almost ready."

He nodded. "Maybe," he agreed, but instead of going upstairs, Blake remained where he was, trying to properly frame what he was about to say. Ordinarily, words were no problem for him, but he had no experience in this area. He wasn't someone given to exposing his feelings. But she obviously needed to be reassured, he thought. "I just want you to know that I enjoyed last night."

Greer took in a long breath, as if that would somehow help her maintain her outer calm. She'd indulged in a breech of protocol last night.

"Yeah, me, too. Doesn't change the fact that I behaved unprofessionally."

Did she think he was going to put her on report? "For the record," he told her, "you 'behaved' just perfectly."

With that, he turned away and walked back toward the stairs, leaving her to contemplate her own thoughts.

Why did life have to be so complicated? Greer wondered, swiftly stirring the eggs that threatened to harden in a clump.

If she'd met Blake under different circumstances, then maybe last night would have been the beginning of something special rather than just an anomaly.

An anomaly, she caught herself thinking as she went to the refrigerator, that she would have dearly loved to have happen again at least one more time before her assignment here ended.

But then—

Greer stopped looking for the butter and drew her head out of the interior of the refrigerator. She could have sworn she'd just heard her name being called.

Was Blake calling her? Or was that—?

No, she was right. She *did* hear Blake calling for her. Again. And there was an urgency in his voice. Oh, damn, what was wrong?

Turning the stove off and moving the large frying pan onto a cool burner, she hurried out of the kitchen. Passing the hall table, she grabbed her handgun, yanking it out of its holster—just in case.

She made it up the stairs in record time.

"Blake?"

Judge, she should have called him Judge, not something as familiar as his first name. She was on duty, for God's sake.

Once blurred, the lines were hard to restore.

"In here!" he called out to her.

Following his voice, not knowing what to expect, she burst into the doorway of the room he was calling from. She held her weapon out in front of her, braced in both hands.

It was his father's room. Blake had the senior

Kincannon on the floor, lying on his back. Blake was in the middle of counting off compressions, one hand pressed on top of the other and both pressing down on the older man's chest. His father was unconscious and Blake was performing CPR.

"Call 911," he cried. "I think he had a heart attack."

Stunned, Greer lost no time in putting in a call to her dispatch at the police station. Giving her badge number, she rattled off the circumstances and the patient's address.

Flipping her phone closed, she tucked it away again. "They'll be here right away," she guaranteed. "They like to keep Aurora's 'finest' in top running condition." She came closer to him. Blake hadn't missed a single beat, performing CPR for all he was worth.

"What happened?" she wanted to know as she looked at his unconscious father on the floor.

Blake shook his head. "I don't know. When he didn't answer my knock, I opened the door and found him like this." He knew that time was of the essence. The quicker his father got treatment, the better his chances for a full recovery would be. "I don't know how long he's been unconscious."

Greer bent down. Pressing two fingers against the other man's throat, she felt for a pulse. It was thin and reedy, but it was there. Relieved, she told Blake, "At least he's still alive."

"Yeah, but I don't know how long he'd been like this," Blake repeated, worried.

"It wasn't all night," she assured him. "When I was

getting my things together to go downstairs, I heard your father moving around in the next bedroom. That had to be some time between one and two."

Blake glanced at his watch as he continued working over his father. "It's six now. What if he's been like this for the past five hours?" he asked. "What if he—"

Greer laid a gentling hand on his shoulder. "Don't get ahead of yourself," she advised sympathetically. Looking at the man on the floor, she thought she saw a slight movement. Greer rallied around it. Slight was better than nothing.

"Look," she pointed out excitedly. "Your father's trying to open his eyes. His eyelashes just fluttered, I'm sure of it!"

Sitting back on his heels, Blake sighed with relief. He'd thought he'd only imagined it. Wishful thinking. But if Greer saw it, too, they couldn't both be hallucinating.

"Thank God," Blake ground out.

There was no masking his pleasure that his father appeared to be coming around and that, with a little bit of luck, was going to be okay. For one awful second, when he'd walked into the room after not receiving any answer to his knock, he'd thought the older man was dead.

The first thing that occurred to him was that Munro had somehow found out his address.

What if the drug dealer had somehow gained access into the house and had killed his father first? He would have never forgiven himself.

But to his relief, a quick check around his father's body showed no blood. There'd been no attack. Immediately something else suggested itself to him. And if that was true, it wasn't exactly a cause for celebration, either.

The words *heart attack* loomed over him with twelve-feet high letters.

Blake knew that his grandfather—his father's father—had died of a heart attack at a relatively young age. Gunny had bragged the other day about already outliving his father. Under normal circumstances, he gave no credence to superstitions, but he didn't believe in thumbing his nose at fate, either.

In the background, the sound of an approaching siren began to register, growing stronger by the second. They'd be here soon, he thought.

"Dad?" Blake cried. He leaned over his father's body, his lips close to the man's ear. "Dad, can you hear me?"

Lips that felt as dry as dust came together in an attempt to form words. When he finally managed, they came out in a whisper.

On her knees on the other side of Blake's father, Greer leaned in to hear what he was trying to tell them. His voice was too low.

"Could you repeat that, Gunny?" Greer asked, her voice deliberately loud.

"Not...deaf..." Gunny told her, his breath just barely sustaining him. He was obviously referring to the fact that his son was fairly shouting when he addressed him.

Shaking his head, Blake blew out a breath. "He's still an ornery old man," he observed. "That's a good sign."

"A very good sign," she agreed, patting his shoulder firmly. Getting up, she moved toward the doorway. "I'll go downstairs and let the paramedics in," she told Blake just before she left.

Blake wasn't sure if he said that was a good idea or if he'd only thought it without actually telling her that. His attention was completely focused on his father's ashen face. And on keeping him alive. "You hang in there, old man. Help's on its way."

"Don't…need…help…just…need…to…rest," Gunny gasped out the words as if each was being wrenched out of him with rusty pliers.

"If you don't want to be resting permanently, old man, you'll accept help," Blake all but ordered him tersely. "I'm not ready to lose you yet, understand?"

"Why? You…got…a…cute…replacement…waiting… in…the…wings," his father said, laboring over each word.

Oh, no, he wasn't about to admit to anything right now. And definitely not to his father. "You don't know what you're talking about, Dad."

He would have smirked if he could have. But he was almost too weak to even draw a single breath. Still, this might be the last conversation he was going to have with his son.

"Saw…her…coming…out…of…your…room…this… morning." Alexander began coughing.

"You *really* don't know what you're talking about, Dad. You're hallucinating," Blake told him. Now wasn't the time to get into this. Once his father was better— and once he knew if what was between the long-legged detective and him had a future, *then* there was time enough to talk about things. Right now, the only thing that mattered was that his father recovered. "Save your breath for something important—like breathing," he ordered.

The next minute, two paramedics came hurrying in. One of them was bringing a gurney. They collapsed it so that it was beside his father.

Rising, Blake moved out of their way, but not so far that he couldn't observe every move that the paramedics made.

"He's going to be all right," Greer told him, her voice confident and firm. For just a second, she rested her hand on his shoulder in mute reassurance.

Blake placed his own hand over hers, as if that could somehow transfuse some of her faith into him. As an unmanageable fear gripped his stomach, Blake only wished he could believe her. But he had always been, first and foremost, a realist and realists knew that everything could change in less than a heartbeat. It had already happened to him once.

Was it happening again?

# Chapter 14

"See, I told you he'd be all right," Greer couldn't resist reminding Blake cheerfully.

It was a little more than twelve hours later and they were finally driving home again. Twelve hours earlier, Blake had ridden in the ambulance with his father and she had followed directly behind them in her car. Thinking ahead, she wanted to ensure that they would have a way home once things settled down.

Once she got a prognosis from the E.R. doctor, Greer contacted the precinct, placing calls to her captain, the chief and Jeff to bring them up to speed on this latest development and to assure all of them that, aside from being worried, the judge was just fine.

Once the danger had passed, they had left his father, alert and complaining, in the coronary care unit on the

first floor of Aurora Memorial, the same hospital whose
fundraiser they had just attended the night before.

It was a small world, Greer remembered thinking
when she'd arrived there and parked her vehicle in the
E.R. lot. The world got even smaller when one of the
cardiologists who had been at that function and had
engaged them in conversation during the evening turned
out to be the doctor who was on call this morning. The
physician wound up treating Blake's father.

Blake was not impressed with her prediction coming
true. Mainly because it hadn't actually *been* a prediction.
"You only said that because that's what people say to
make other people feel better in dire times."

"No," she contradicted, easing down on the brake
as she approached a red light, "I said that because I
really felt your father was going to be all right. Gunny's
strong as an ox and, for the most part, he eats rather
healthy."

"For the past three weeks," he agreed, then told her,
"That's all on you. Until you started cooking, takeout
was all either one of us had had for the past couple of
years. In my father's case, probably a lot longer."

She'd thought the takeout thing was just a temporary
aberration. To think of two grown, capable men having
nothing else but whatever food they could have brought
to their door was mind-boggling.

"Seriously?"

Blake laughed shortly. "Seriously. You've made changes
in his life. In our lives," he amended, then abruptly stopped.
Maybe he'd said too much. He wasn't sure if he was ready
to make these kinds of admissions yet.

"Nice to know," she murmured, more to herself than to him. Foot on the accelerator again, she switched lanes to move faster than the beige Cadillac in front of them. "Your father should be fine and back on his feet in a couple of days."

That was the projection the doctor had made, as well, but Blake wasn't buying into it wholeheartedly. "If that's the case, why wouldn't they let me take my father home again? Why are they keeping him in CCU?"

She knew the answer to that. "They're just following standard procedure. Everyone experiencing 'an episode,'" she told him, referring to the heart attack his father'd had in the neutral terms that doctors used, "is kept in CCU for twenty-four hours because the doctors want to observe the patient, make sure nothing else is going on that could prove fatal."

It sounded to him as if Greer knew what she was talking about. "I take it you've been through this before?"

She nodded grimly. "One of the detectives in the squad, a guy by the name of Ray Walker." She always felt a story sounded more real and personal if the people in it had names. "The man should have retired long ago except that he had nothing to retire to except four walls and silence. So he managed to convince the chief to let him stay a little while longer. Well, one day he tried to chase down a perp over half his age and had one of those 'episodes.' Luckily, the ambulance attendants rushed him to this hospital."

She'd gotten him curious. "This Detective Walker, he still working at the precinct?"

Greer shook her head. "With such a recent history of heart trouble, the brass *made* him retire. They didn't want to hear any excuses."

He knew of former judges, devoid of any hobbies to hold their interest, who just seemed to fade away once they retired. Their lives seemingly without purpose, they died less than a year after they left the bench. In one case, it was more like two months.

"How did this detective handle his retirement?"

Greer smiled then. "Not too badly—I gave him one of Hussy's puppies so that he'd have something warm and loving licking his face each morning when he woke up." She'd visited Walker just before landing this assignment. Master and dog were doing just fine. Nothing could have pleased her more. "Seems to have worked out well for everyone."

Nodding, Blake put his own spin on the story. "So you moonlight as a terminal do-gooder?"

She'd never cared for the term "do-gooder" but she wasn't averse to the actual act. "Hey, life's hard enough as it is. No reason we can't make it a little more bearable for the people we interact with if we can."

Margaret would have liked this woman, he couldn't help thinking. They would have probably become good friends. The thought made him relax a little and allow his guard to slip again.

He thought of the past few weeks and said, "Well, you certainly made it more bearable for my father." And then, because that wasn't all, he lowered his voice and added, "And for me."

There it went again, she suddenly realized. Her pulse was accelerating just because the man had lowered his voice. Hearing it had made her imagination take off and she found herself thinking about last night. About every glorious second of lovemaking that had taken place between them.

She couldn't keep doing this to herself, Greer thought fiercely. She *knew* this wasn't the kind of thing that had a prayer of lasting. It was too overwhelming, too hot. And things that were too hot never remained that way. They cooled, returning to normal.

This was all happening because she and Blake were in an artificial setting which amounted to a highly volatile life-and-death situation. Once the threat, the urgency, was gone and life leveled off, so would his reaction to her. The level of passion and excitement that had exploded between them wasn't the kind of thing that had a long shelf life. It was evaluated in terms of days, not months or years. She *knew* that.

So why did she find herself praying that this could be the one exception?

For now, she had to stop torturing herself and put it out of her mind. She might be an optimist, but she'd stopped believing in Santa Claus a long time ago and believing that this relationship had a shot at outliving the dramatic set of circumstances they found themselves came under that heading.

They were here, at his development, and she wasn't a hundred percent sure how they'd gotten here. She needed to keep tighter control over her thoughts.

As they drove onto Kincannon's street, she saw that

there were parked cars all up and down both sides of the block, spilling out onto the next one. She heard the music and the noise of loud voices trying to talk over one another coming from the house next door to Blake's.

*This can't be good.*

Greer slowed her own vehicle down as she passed by the squad car where the two patrolmen charged with the task of watching the judge's house were parked.

"What's going on?" Blake asked them before Greer had a chance to.

"Someone in the house next to yours is having a birthday party, Your Honor," the officer behind the steering wheel told him. "There was a delivery truck here earlier. Never saw so many balloons in my life."

"The cake was huge, too," the second policeman put in with enthusiasm. "Made you hungry just looking at it."

The first man gave him an annoyed look for interrupting. "Everything makes you hungry." He turned back to face Blake. "People started arriving about the same time. Want one of us to talk to them about keeping the noise level down?" It was obvious that he was dying to do just that.

Greer glanced toward Blake, leaving the matter up to him. He shook his head.

"It's not so bad. Maybe they'll wear themselves out and wind down." Blake glanced at the clock in the dashboard. "Besides, it's only eight o'clock." Although disturbing the peace wasn't attached to any particular time, most people didn't register complaints about noise levels until after eleven. He saw no reason to do any differently.

The first patrolman looked slightly embarrassed. "When it's dark like this, I keep thinking it's later. How's your father, sir?"

"Doctor said he's going to be just fine. Thanks for asking," Blake replied.

Both officers smiled at the news. "Glad to hear that, sir," the more heavyset one said.

He wanted to get inside, to unwind and relax. With Greer. Blake nodded at the two patrolmen. "Well, good night, Officers."

Greer took her cue and drove on. Parking the car in Blake's driveway, she got out and waited for him to lead the way to the front door.

The noise coming from the house next door seemed to all but surround them now. Several people had spilled out of the house, clutching chunky glasses in their hands they would pause to sip from on a regular basis.

"Sure you don't want Officer Hogan to talk to your neighbors about the noise level?" she asked, leaning into him so he could hear her without having to raise her voice. What she did manage to raise, though, was her body temperature. That seemed to be the case every time she was closer than skin to him. And it was only getting more pronounced with each time.

But Blake shook his head and stood by his decision. "It's nice to hear some celebratory noise right about now," he told her. He looked over the lawn to the next house. "I've half a mind to join them."

As far as she could see, there was no reason not

to if that was what he really wanted. "We could," she told him.

"No," he contradicted with a smile, "we couldn't. I don't even know what my neighbor looks like." He'd been too busy, too caught up in trying to work as hard as he could to keep from thinking about Margaret, to meet any of his neighbors. "I wouldn't presume to crash his party. Until this threat came along, I'd even forgotten there were sunrises and sunsets."

Greer frowned, puzzled. In the background, one of the guests, a young teenage girl, shrieked with glee, then ran off, eluding the grasp of a teenage boy. "The threat did that for you?"

"No," he answered quietly, his eyes on hers. "You did."

"Oh, don't sweet-talk me, Judge." She was only half teasing. It was getting harder and harder to remind herself that this wasn't going to go anywhere. That their relationship had no hope of surviving once this assignment ended. "It makes my insides all melty. I'm not much good to you with a melty center."

Blake ran the back of his knuckles very slowly along her cheek, caressing her. "Oh, I don't know about that. There's something to be said for a woman who's tough on the outside, tender on the inside."

She grinned, doing her best to remain strong. "Funny, that same description could also be used to describe a steak."

Blake laughed softly under his breath as he disarmed his security system long enough for them to enter. "My favorite meat," he acknowledged.

Nothing she liked better than prime rib, nice and rare. "Mine, too."

His smile was swiftly decimating her. "Something else we have in common."

There was no point in tallying their similarities. It would only make the inevitable that much more difficult to bear when it happened. The only thing that mattered was that she continue doing her job, continue keeping Blake safe.

They were in the foyer and she needed to go through her routine, checking each room to make sure it was secure. Home security systems were all well and good, but even the finest system could be bypassed if the person attempting entry was clever enough.

"Stay right here," she told him, nodding to where he stood, "while I check out the house and make sure that it's secure."

"Don't you think that's a little over the top?" he asked her.

"Why?" She saw no reason to change her methods of operation this late in the game. "It's what I do every night when we come home from the courthouse. Things happen. Jeff said they were closing in on Munro and his people." Her partner had given her an update when she'd called him about Alexander's heart attack. "A man gets desperate at times like that. He must know that his number's up and that he's living on borrowed time. If he wants to hurt you, now would be the time to do it."

"But there's been a police patrol car across the street ever since we left for the hospital," he pointed out.

It was true, but none of that mattered. "Lots of ways

for a creative man to gain access. Don't you know that every time they build a better mouse trap, someone builds an even better mouse?"

"Strictly speaking," he corrected her with an indulgent smile, "mice aren't built, they're made."

"Same difference," she told him, undaunted. "Stay right here," she repeated. "This isn't going to take long."

He had no intention of standing here in the foyer like some hapless silent movie heroine, waiting for Greer to sweep through the area and declare it safe. "Haven't you learned yet that the fastest way to make me come with you is to tell me not to?"

The other times, he'd had his father to talk to when he'd come home. Now he had only his concerns to keep him company. "I'll move faster if you're not with me," she told him.

He sighed, giving in. "All right, but hurry this along," Blake urged her. "I have definite plans for tonight."

She drew her weapon. "Work?"

"Only in the broadest sense of the definition," he told her and she could hear the smile in his voice. "Actually, I'd say it was more along the lines of pleasure."

The living room was clear. She moved on to the kitchen, crossing the floor in short, measured steps as she remained on high alert.

"Oh?" She spared one glance over her shoulder in his direction. "Would you care to be a little more specific than that?"

His eyes were laughing at her. He was obviously enjoying himself. "Not really."

"Don't want to share with the class?" she asked, amused. "What happened to 'works well and plays well with others'?"

She heard him chuckle to himself. "Depends on who those 'others' are."

She stopped abruptly and for a moment, Greer lowered her weapon, as well as her guard. "Me, Blake. Me."

"I suppose I can arrange to give you a small, intimate preview," he allowed. Moving the hand that was holding the gun aside, he took Greer into his arms.

No, she couldn't allow herself to be sidetracked, Greer silently insisted. No matter how much she wanted to.

"Judge—"

"Blake," he corrected her, his voice low and seductive. Now that his father was out of danger, all he could think about was making love with Greer. All night long. "Don't backslide on me now, Greer. You were doing so well." His lips covered hers.

Her head was spinning and her pulse had already taken off. She could feel her body temperature rising. She struggled to hold desire back until she completed her check. With effort, she wedged her hands up against his chest and pushed him back.

"We shouldn't be doing this," she insisted.

"And yet, we are," he told her.

And then he kissed her again and her resolve all but went up in smoke. She wanted nothing more than to spend the night in his arms, completely lost.

But her training, her dedication to the job, all but screamed for her not to be derelict in her duties. She couldn't just throw caution to the wind, that wasn't her, that wasn't how she was wired. She was the one who had to put her life on the line for Blake. She was the one who very possibly stood between the man and a fatal bullet.

Damn it, she needed to stop thinking of herself, of the pleasure that he'd brought her in so many different ways. The only thing that was important was keeping him safe.

Time to start acting like the cop she was, she reminded herself.

For the second time, she put her hands on Blake's chest and pushed hard. She couldn't think, couldn't do her job, with his lips on hers. She needed to pull back while she still could.

"Blake, please, I need to make sure the locks are all secure on the windows and that if someone tries to come in, the alarm will go off."

The last thing on his mind were intruders. Blake shrugged away her suggestion. No one had tried to gain access to his house in the three-plus weeks she'd been here. There was no reason to think that tonight had been any different.

But he knew the futility of arguing with her. Sighing, he nodded, surrendering. "Do what you have to do."

She let out a shaky breath. God, but that man could scramble her brain faster than anyone she'd ever known. "Glad you see things my way."

He shrugged. As if there was a choice. "Is there any other way?"

"No," she agreed, "but it's nice to have you so agreeable."

The family room was next. Wide open, she cleared it in a moment.

Someone shrieked next door. Greer's head jerked in that direction, listening.

Was that good or bad? The noise, though muffled by concrete and wood, was swelling.

Again, she toyed with the idea of having the patrolmen ask the neighbors to keep it down to a friendly roar. All that noise was making her uneasy. Munro or anyone he sent in his place could easily use the party next door as cover. There were so many people there, it would be easy to just blend in and camouflage himself with the noise.

The thought made her more uneasy.

What if one of Munro's henchmen had already done that? Had already blended in with the party guests just long enough to gain access to the neighbors' backyard and then slipped inside Blake's house? It wouldn't be all that difficult do.

Her heart pounded as she examined the idea.

"Why don't you put some champagne on ice?" she suggested just before she went to check the second floor.

Making her way up the stairs, Greer took out her cell phone. She had no idea why, but her gut kept telling her that something was off. Maybe the party next door was making her nervous, she wasn't sure. But she knew she'd feel better if she had Carson around. Two sets of eyes were better than one.

Pressing the single key that connected her to her partner, she wound up listening to an answering machine. Damn, it was Saturday night. Why did she think Jeff was going to be home or somewhere where he could actually hear his phone when it rang?

Greer almost terminated the call, but then decided, since she'd called, she might as well leave a message. Otherwise, he'd quiz her about the aborted call and more likely than not, drive her crazy by putting his own less-than-upstanding spin on it.

"Jeff, this is Greer. Call me when you get this," she told the answering machine. "I think I might need backup here. I'm at the judge's house."

Finished, she put the phone back into her pocket. Closing the door to the bathroom after a quick peek, she opened Blake's bedroom door next.

And found herself staring down the barrel of a Glock.

"About time you got home, Cinderella."

Her heart froze.

Munro.

# Chapter 15

"**D**rop your gun," Munro snarled as he raised his weapon, aiming it dead center at her heart.

Damn it, when was she going to learn to trust her gut? Greer admonished herself. She'd *sensed* that there was something wrong.

Adrenaline launched through her veins in double time. Rather than drop her gun, she mimicked his action and raised it so that, if fired, the bullet would create a hole in his chest.

"The way I see it," she said to Munro, her voice deadly calm, "our guns cancel each other out."

"Well, I don't see it that way," he snapped back. "Now drop your gun or my 'associate' in the next room drops your judge."

It was a five-dollar word coming out of a two-bit mouth. Munro's conceit was incredible. He actually thought he was going to get away with this, with killing a judge and a narcotic detective right under the noses of the Aurora police.

"You don't have an 'associate' in the next room, Munro," she said in the same calm voice, knowing it annoyed the hell out of the dealer. She knew he wanted her to cower, to show fear. "Nobody wants to 'associate' with a lowlife like you."

Steely, lifeless brown eyes locked onto hers. She could feel her blood run cold. This was a man who could kill without the slightest qualm.

"They don't, huh?" Munro taunted. "You confident enough to put that little theory of yours to the test, bitch?"

If this involved just her, she would have met what she felt was his bluff in a heartbeat. But it wasn't just about her. Even if she hadn't gotten so involved with Blake that he dominated her every waking thought, the man was first and foremost her responsibility and she couldn't take a chance that this cocky little bastard *wasn't* bluffing.

A malevolent smile curved his mouth. It was as if he was privy to her thought process. "Two seconds to make up your mind, bitch, and then that good judge of yours is history."

In her experience there were criminals who had a small amount of redeeming qualities about them. Munro didn't number among them.

"He's history anyway," she responded. The drug dealer had vowed to kill Kincannon. She had no reason to believe that Munro had changed his mind.

"Maybe. Maybe not," Munro allowed in a singsong voice, twisting his wrist and moving the plane of his gun—but not the barrel—as he spoke. "He cost me a lot of revenue when he cleaned up the streets, putting my regular customers behind bars. Maybe I'd be satisfied ransoming Kincannon back to the justice system that thinks so highly of him. We could call it 'reparations.'" His small mouth curved further in an evil smile that all but froze her blood. "What do you think of that?"

Greer continued to hold her weapon trained on his chest. "What do I think? I think that you're lying."

"Not as dumb as you look," he assessed, laughing to himself. It sounded a little like the sound a hyena made. "Still, I could use the money. Besides, the damn bastard's hard to kill. I know. I've tried. Got his wife, but not him. Lucky son of a bitch," he commented.

Her eyes widened. "You were the one who ran him off the road?"

He smirked at her naiveté. "Hey, I got people."

What he meant, she realized, was that he had someone do his dirty work for him. "I forgot, you're a big operator."

The smile faded as if he understood she was being sarcastic. "Yeah, I am. Now put that damn thing down," he ordered. A hint of the cold smile returned. "Or shoot me. The second you pull that trigger, there'll be another shot and the judge'll be dead. He doesn't have a gun like you do," he mocked her. "C'mon, Detective." He tapped the watch on the wrist of his gun hand. "Tick-tock."

Greer was torn. God help her, she couldn't take a chance.

"All right," she fairly shouted, raising her voice so that it would carry, either to Blake or the so-called other gunman in the house. "You win." Moving in slow motion, she lowered her weapon and placed it on the floor before her.

His unnerving smile widened at the word *win*. "Never saw it happening any other way. Kick the damn thing over here. Now!" he ordered when she made no move to do as he said.

"Greer, what's taking you so long?"

It was Blake. He sounded as if he was close by. There *was* no other gunman she realized, cursing herself.

The next moment, Blake walked into the bedroom. And stopped dead.

She'd been played, Greer thought, furious. The second she'd realized that, she knew exactly what Munro's next move was going to be. To kill Blake.

There were two ways to go. She could either dive for her weapon or throw herself over Blake and take the bullet she knew with certainty was coming. There was no time to dive for the gun and get Munro.

Greer did the only thing she could, she threw her body in front of Blake, at the same time crying, "My thigh," to him and praying he understood.

Everything happened in a blur.

By throwing herself on Blake, Greer managed to get him out of the line of fire.

But not without a price.

Munro's shot went into her shoulder, even as Blake, grabbing her, tried to twist her away and push her beneath him.

As she went down, Greer felt Blake's hands grope under her skirt and knew he'd understood. He'd secured her smaller, secondary weapon, pulling it free of its holster. From the floor, he shot straight up, getting off a shot that miraculously went straight into Munro's neck.

Blood spurted as the latter tried to shriek. The sound came out a guttural gurgle. Trying to stop the flow of blood with his hands, Munro sank down to his knees, then fell over.

Groggy, light-headed, Greer crawled over to the fallen drug dealer, putting her own hands over the hole in his neck. She needed to stem the flow before he bled out. Right now, it seemed next to impossible.

"911," she cried out to Blake, pressing the heel of her hand against the hole. "Call 911."

Blake was already on his cell phone, giving the pertinent information to the dispatcher on the other end of the line. Finished, he dropped his cell phone on the bed and focused his attention on Greer, not the man most likely dying in his bedroom.

That was when he saw the blood all along her shoulder and arm. "You're bleeding," he cried, horrified.

"I am?" She was still feeling numb, detached from her own body. Disoriented, Greer looked down at her torso. He was right, she thought. That had to be her blood, not Munro's. Taking a deep breath, she could now feel her insides beginning to shake. She didn't have time for this.

Her eyes swept over Blake. No blood. Good. "Are you all right?" she asked him.

"I'm fine," he snapped. Blake was angry at himself for not coming upstairs sooner. Angrier still when he thought that he might have lost her altogether. He wanted to hold Greer but he was afraid to touch her, afraid that he would only make things worse and hurt her. "Damn it, Greer, when are you going to learn you're not a human shield?"

"Easy. When you stop having people shoot at you." It took effort to talk. Her strength seemed to be deserting her at an alarming rate.

Was it her imagination, or was that the sound of sirens in the background?

"Do you think maybe you could take over?" she asked Blake, laboring over each word. "I'm not sure I can press down hard enough."

He looked down at the man who for almost the past four weeks had been such a threat to him. He didn't look so foreboding now. Eddie Munro's eyes were staring lifelessly at the ceiling. Blake bent down and felt for a pulse. There was none.

"I don't think any amount of pressure is going to help, Greer," he told her gently. "Munro's dead." Blake took another look at her shoulder. It appeared worse than he'd first thought. Blood was oozing down her arm. "You're the one who needs to have pressure applied to her wound."

As if in denial of his assessment, Greer rose shakily to her feet.

"No, I'm fine," she protested, but her voice sounded reedy and thin to her ear.

That was when the light-headedness really caught

up to her. She was vaguely aware of people coming into the room as the room began to spin. And then, abruptly, the people seemed to disappear, fading off into nothingness.

The fire in her shoulder overwhelmed her at the same time the rest of the room vanished.

When Greer regained consciousness, for a moment she had no recollection of what had happened, no idea what day it was or where she was. The scene around her came into focus by degrees.

She was aware of motion, of a faintly antiseptic smell and of someone holding her hand tightly. Greer had the faint sense that if whoever it was let go, she would wind up floating away.

Opening her eyes, she saw that Blake was sitting beside her. He was the one holding her hand so tightly.

Someone she didn't recognize was next to him. It took her another couple of seconds to realize that the man was a paramedic.

What had happened? How had she gotten here?

"Welcome back," Blake said, relief and emotion drenching every syllable.

She raised her head. The effort caused a herd of buffalo to pound their hooves across her forehead. She dropped her head back down. The swaying motion was making her nauseous. "Am I in an ambulance?"

"Yes," Blake answered.

She didn't belong in an ambulance. She had a report to write up. "Why?"

"Because the hospital is too far away for me to run there with you in my arms," Blake informed her simply.

"I don't need a hospital," Greer protested. She tried to get up again only to have him push her back down. It didn't require much effort on his part and that *really* upset her.

"You need a keeper," Blake told her, "but a hospital'll do for now."

"You're very lucky, Detective," the paramedic chimed in. "A little bit to the left and it would have gone through your heart. And you would have been on your way to the coroner instead."

"Lucky," Greer murmured. The buffalo herd was fading, but her head was beginning to spin big-time.

She was going to pass out again, she thought.

Greer tightened her grasp on Blake's hand, or at least tried to. She felt weaker than a day-old kitten. "Don't go anywhere," she whispered to Blake.

"Wasn't planning on it," he assured her with barely harnessed feeling.

She only heard the first word.

"They want you to stay overnight to be observed," Blake told her as she struggled to get dressed. He was torn between helping her and forcing her to remain. From where he stood, it would take very little strength for the latter.

It was several hours later. The E.R. physician had removed the bullet, cleaned out her wound and bandaged it. And while she was waiting for all that to happen, in between the tests they'd forced her to take, she'd told Blake about what Munro had said to her when they were alone. That he was the one behind the car accident that had killed his wife.

The news had stunned him into silence for a few moments. But then, to her amazement, Blake seemed to take it in stride and said the debt had been paid. Munro was dead.

"I really think you should listen and stay overnight," he pressed. He had come very close to losing her tonight. It brought home to him just how much he'd come to care for this woman fate had brought into his life for a second time.

"I don't want to be observed," Greer insisted. "I'm fine, except for the hole in my shoulder."

"And the blood loss," Blake patiently pointed out.

"Being manufactured and replaced even as we speak," she assured him cheerfully.

She looked down at the pantyhose in her hand. There was no way she was going to be able to get them on. With a half shrug, she stuffed them into the purse that was resting on the bed.

Blake pulled the purse away from her. "Damn it, woman, are you always going to be this stubborn?"

The answer required no thought. "Pretty much. But you don't have to worry about that." It was an effort to sound cheerful, but she'd already promised herself that when this moment came, she wasn't going to give in to emotion, wasn't going to wish that they had longer. It was what it was and now it was time to move on. For both of them. "With Munro dead, looks like you're about to get your life back."

"Yeah," Blake agreed, his voice flat. He blew out a breath. *Now or never.* "What if I told you I don't want it back?"

She stopped struggling with the buttons on her shirt. "I'm not following you. You liked being threatened?"

"I've discovered that I like the side effects of being threatened." She was still looking at him as if he was delivering a lecture in a foreign language. Frustrated, Blake blew out another breath. "Damn it, Greer, do I have to spell it out for you?"

"That might be nice," she responded. "My brain's a little fuzzy right now. I'm liable to think the wrong thing."

She was doing this on purpose, he thought. "This doesn't come easy for me."

"Someone once told me that nothing worthwhile is ever easy. Or maybe that was on the inside of a fortune cookie, I'm not sure." She ran a hand across her forehead. She was still a little light-headed, this time from the painkillers they'd give her while working on her shoulder. "It's all kind of muddled."

"Okay, I'll spell it out." If he had to, so be it. "But before I do, you have to promise me that you're going to stop throwing yourself on top of me."

Her grin was wicked. "I thought you liked that part."

That wasn't it and she knew it. "Not when there's gunfire involved."

He seemed to be missing a very salient point. "If

I hadn't thrown myself in front of you, Munro would have killed you—and you wouldn't have been able to get my backup weapon," she pointed out. "Nice shot, by the way." She stopped struggling with her clothes and paused to look at him. "You didn't tell me you knew your way around firearms."

He would have thought that was a given, considering his background. "Knowing my way around guns is part of having a father who spent his life as a marine. If you want your dad to pay attention to you, you pay attention to what *he* pays attention to." Not to mention that, for the first time in his life, he was grateful for the career his father had chosen.

"And you're changing the subject," Blake accused. If he was going to say this, he needed to say it now, before his courage flagged. "Don't take this the wrong way, but please just shut up and listen." His hand on her good arm, he forced her to sit down again. "I don't want my old life back," he repeated. "I want the new one, the one that I've been living with you."

She raised her eyes to his face but said nothing.

The silence got to be too much for him. Why wasn't she saying anything? Was he wrong? He'd felt sure that she felt about him the way he did about her, but now— "Say something."

"You told me to shut up and listen," she reminded him innocently.

"Now I'm telling you to talk."

She didn't want to get swept away, didn't want to risk her heart. "You want to keep on seeing me?"

"In a word, yes. But I want to do more than that."

"More than see me," she repeated. "You want to touch me?" she asked, humor curving her mouth.

"I want to marry you."

She wasn't prepared for that.

The air rushed out of her lungs. It took Greer more than a few seconds to recover and pull herself together. Her first reaction was to want to throw her arms around his neck and cry, "Yes," but she knew better. No matter how much she wanted to, she couldn't believe him. Couldn't let herself get carried away.

"You don't mean that," she told him quietly.

"Yes, I do," he insisted. He'd never meant anything more in his life. Especially now after what she'd told him about Margaret. Life changed in a heartbeat. He wanted his heart beating next to hers for as long as they both had.

Greer shook her head. "That's just the adrenaline talking," she insisted, hating every word she was uttering. "We've just gone through a life-and-death situation. Our whole relationship is based on a life-and-death scenario. You're not up to making any rational decisions right now."

The hell he wasn't. "I know what I feel, Greer," he told her firmly. "I'm in love with you."

But Greer refused to be swayed. "No, you know what you *think* you feel. In a week, when you're back in your courtroom, going about your daily routine, you won't feel the way you do right now."

Blake turned the tables on her. "And what is it that *you* feel?" He waited, knowing that her answer was the crucial one. That his whole fate hung in the balance.

If she told him she didn't love him, it would change everything. Not the way he felt about her, but it would change the scheme of the future he was envisioning.

That wasn't the point, Greer thought. "What I feel doesn't matter, Blake."

He took her hand, forcing her to look into his eyes. "It does to me."

She loved him. It had hit her like a ton of bricks when she thought Munro was going to kill him. She was willing to die in his place, not because it was her job, but because she loved him and wanted him to live no matter what.

He was still waiting, she thought. Waiting for her to tell him how she felt. "I can't tell you."

Blake didn't understand. "Why not?"

"Because you'll just use it against my argument." She watched as the smile unfurled on his lips a fraction at a time until it seemed to take over his entire face. "Don't grin at me like that."

"Why not?" He slipped his arm around her and drew her closer to him. "You all but admitted that you love me."

"We're not talking about how I feel about you, we're talking about you."

"We're talking about *us*," he corrected. "And you're wrong, this isn't adrenaline, or something that's just part of a temporary rush. I've been in love before, Greer. I know exactly what it feels like. It feels good. It feels right. The only rush I get is when you're in my arms, when I'm kissing you, when I'm making love with you.

No guns are involved then. Now, once and for all, do you or don't you love me?" he pressed.

He had her back to the wall. There was no way she could lie.

"I love you," she admitted. But as he moved to kiss her, she put her hand on his chest, holding him in place. "I'd still rather you took time to let the situation cool off."

"I can if you want me to," he agreed. "But the feeling will still be the same." He took her free hand in both of his. "None of us know how much time we have. Today is all there might be. I don't want to waste a single minute away from you. I don't want to put my life on hold anymore. I don't want to get myself lost in my work." The way he had when Margaret died. "The only 'getting lost' I want to do is with you. Now, we can wait if you want to—because I sure as hell don't—or you can give me your answer now and we can go home and start planning the rest of our life together. The choice is yours."

She wasn't that sure about that. "And if I say wait?"

He sighed. "Then I'll wait. Not patiently," he promised, kissing first her lips, then her forehead, then the hollow of her throat. "But I'll wait."

He knew it made her crazy when he littered her skin with small, tantalizing kisses like that, she thought. Despite everything she'd been through tonight, her pulse was racing again. The man had some kind of magic power over her, there was no other way to describe it.

"You don't play fair," she groaned, feeling herself begin to melt.

He laughed, kissing the side of her neck. "Playing fair wasn't part of the initial deal."

She was breathing hard and definitely not thinking clearly. But she was rejoicing. Every single inch of her was rejoicing.

"Yes," she breathed.

"How's that again?"

"Yes," she repeated with effort, "I'll marry you."

He laughed as triumph soared through him. "That's all I wanted to hear." He got off the bed, still holding her hand. "Let's go home."

"In a second." Standing up next to him, Greer wrapped her good arm around his neck, leaned against him and sealed the bargain with a heated kiss that promised to go on for a very long time.

Which was just fine with both of them.

\* \* \* \* \*

*Don't miss Marie Ferrarella's next romance,*
COLTON BY MARRIAGE,
*the first book in the exciting new*
*THE COLTONS OF MONTANA continuity*
*from Silhouette Romantic Suspense.*
*Available June 29, 2010.*

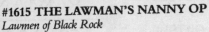

# COMING NEXT MONTH

## Available June 29, 2010

ROMANTIC SUSPENSE

# REQUEST YOUR FREE BOOKS!

## 2 FREE NOVELS PLUS 2 FREE GIFTS!

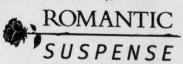

### Silhouette®
# ROMANTIC
# SUSPENSE
*Sparked by Danger, Fueled by Passion.*

**YES!** Please send me 2 FREE Silhouette® Romantic Suspense novels and my 2 FREE gifts (gifts are worth about $10). After receiving them, if I don't wish to receive any more books, I can return the shipping statement marked "cancel." If I don't cancel, I will receive 4 brand-new novels every month and be billed just $4.24 per book in the U.S. or $4.99 per book in Canada. That's a saving of 15% off the cover price! It's quite a bargain! Shipping and handling is just 50¢ per book.* I understand that accepting the 2 free books and gifts places me under no obligation to buy anything. I can always return a shipment and cancel at any time. Even if I never buy another book from Silhouette, the two free books and gifts are mine to keep forever.

240/340 SDN E5Q4

| | |
|---|---|
| Name | (PLEASE PRINT) |
| Address | Apt. # |
| City | State/Prov. | Zip/Postal Code |

Signature (if under 18, a parent or guardian must sign)

### Mail to the Silhouette Reader Service:
**IN U.S.A.:** P.O. Box 1867, Buffalo, NY 14240-1867
**IN CANADA:** P.O. Box 609, Fort Erie, Ontario L2A 5X3

Not valid for current subscribers to Silhouette Romantic Suspense books.

**Want to try two free books from another line?**
**Call 1-800-873-8635 or visit www.morefreebooks.com.**

\* Terms and prices subject to change without notice. Prices do not include applicable taxes. N.Y. residents add applicable sales tax. Canadian residents will be charged applicable provincial taxes and GST. Offer not valid in Quebec. This offer is limited to one order per household. All orders subject to approval. Credit or debit balances in a customer's account(s) may be offset by any other outstanding balance owed by or to the customer. Please allow 4 to 6 weeks for delivery. Offer available while quantities last.

**Your Privacy:** Silhouette is committed to protecting your privacy. Our Privacy Policy is available online at www.eHarlequin.com or upon request from the Reader Service. From time to time we make our lists of customers available to reputable third parties who may have a product or service of interest to you. If you would prefer we not share your name and address, please check here. ☐

**Help us get it right**—We strive for accurate, respectful and relevant communications. To clarify or modify your communication preferences, visit us at www.ReaderService.com/consumerschoice.

SRS10R

# HARLEQUIN®

## A Romance

### FOR EVERY MOOD™

Spotlight on

## — Heart & Home —

Heartwarming romances
where love can happen
right when you least expect it.

See the next page to enjoy a sneak peek
from Silhouette Special Edition®,
a Heart and Home series.

*Introducing* MCFARLANE'S PERFECT BRIDE
*by* USA TODAY *bestselling author Christine Rimmer,*
*from Silhouette Special Edition®.*

Entranced. Captivated. Enchanted.

Connor sat across the table from Tori Jones and
couldn't help thinking that those words exactly described
what effect the small-town schoolteacher had on him.
He might as well stop trying to tell himself he wasn't
interested. He was powerfully drawn to her.

Clearly, he should have dated more when he was
younger.

There had been a couple of other women since Jennifer
had walked out on him. But he had never been entranced.
Or captivated. Or enchanted.

Until now.

He wanted her—*her*, Tori Jones, in particular. Not just
someone suitably attractive and well-bred, as Jennifer had
been. Not just someone sophisticated, sexually exciting
and discreet, which pretty much described the two women
he'd dated after his marriage crashed and burned.

It came to him that he...he *liked* this woman. And that
was new to him. He liked her quick wit, her wisdom and
her big heart. He liked the passion in her voice when she
talked about things she believed in.

He liked *her.* And suddenly it mattered all out of
proportion that she might like him, too.

Was he losing it? He couldn't help but wonder. Was
he cracking under the strain—of the soured economy, the
McFarlane House setbacks, his divorce, the scary changes
in his son? Of the changes he'd decided he needed to make
in his life and himself?

Strangely, right then, on his first date with Tori Jones, he didn't care if he just might be going over the edge. He was having a great time—having *fun*, of all things—and he didn't want it to end.

*Is Connor finally able to admit his feelings to Tori, and are they reciprocated?*
*Find out in McFARLANE'S PERFECT BRIDE*
*by* USA TODAY *bestselling author Christine Rimmer.*
*Available July 2010,*
*only from Silhouette Special Edition®.*

SSEEXP0710

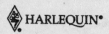